Mistletoe and Meows

12 Cats of Christmas Romance - book 3

Karen Drew

K.E. O'Connor Books

MISTLETOE AND MEOWS

ISBN: 978-1-915378-23-1

Written by: Karen Drew

Chapter 1

Gabe

"You look like a jerk dressed as a Christmas elf. Aren't you too old to play dress up?" Ernie snatched the wrapped gift away from me and scowled at it as if it might explode in his hand.

"Happy Christmas to you too, buddy," I said.

Ernie's frown deepened, and he shook the box. He didn't have much to smile about, having to spend Christmas in a shelter for the homeless.

I patted him on the arm. It was only a small gesture of kindness, just like the gift.

"It had better not be socks. All the so called good samaritans keep turning up with socks. How many feet do they think I have?"

"It gets cold out. Socks are a great gift. And you need to keep warm. It's been below freezing these last few nights. I reckon we'll get new snow fall before Christmas Day." I adjusted my pointed ears.

Ernie grunted. "I'll take a bottle of whiskey if you've got any in that sack of yours. That'll keep the chill out."

I chuckled as I sorted through the gifts. "No alcohol. Besides, you're on a winning streak. How long has it been?"

"Six months, two weeks, three days," Ernie checked his battered watch, "and twelve hours."

"You'll soon be getting your one year sober token."

"And I'll celebrate with a glass of water. Whoopee do-dah!"

"Enjoy your socks, Ernie." I hoisted the sack over my shoulder and headed to the next gift deposit site.

Pete and Archie were ahead of me, singing out of tune Christmas songs as they carried their loaded sacks of donated presents.

I rounded the corner and spotted half a dozen regulars waiting for our arrival. They all knew the drill and where to find us if they wanted clean socks, warm hats, and other practical things to keep them going at this harsh time of year.

A group of us volunteered to do the Christmas gift drop off for the street homeless every December in Silver Birch. I made the trip back home especially for this. But this year was different. This year, I wasn't planning on leaving.

A curvy woman dressed in a long red coat, a hat with a bobble pulled down over her ears, walked toward the group, pushing a bright pink pram with silver tinsel wrapped around the handles. She stopped and spoke to the homeless guys.

I raised an eyebrow. Most women on their own would cross the road and avoid them, thinking they could get in trouble.

Several of them looked in the pram, smiles on their weather-beaten faces. Two of the guys laughed and nudged each other.

I frowned at their response. Why were they laughing at the baby?

Archie and Pete's arrival distracted the group, and they left the woman alone and headed over to receive their Christmas gifts.

The woman stood watching the gifts get handed out for a few seconds, a smile on her face.

I walked over to her and tilted my head. There was something familiar about that cute button nose and those plump cheeks that were bright pink from the biting cold.

"Hey! I don't think you need anything from our Christmas sacks, do you?" I said.

She glanced my way. Her flushed cheeks grew even pinker and her large, dark eyes widened. "Oh! No, I don't need help. I'm not homeless." She looked down at her coat. "Do I look homeless to you?"

"Nope. You look great. I'm Gabe." I nodded, grinning as I took in her poker straight blonde hair sticking out from under the hat, curves in all the right places, and those deep, mysterious eyes. And those lips. They were possibly the most kissable I'd ever seen.

She simply nodded, not giving out her name.

Okay, mysterious lady, you can be coy. Coy and seriously cute.

"I've been doing the Christmas homeless present drop for five years. I come back every year to help at St. Peter's Church," I said.

Her full lips pursed. "That's good of you. Not many people are charitable to those who find themselves on the street. I feel sorry for them. My toes go numb just imagining sleeping rough."

"Yeah, these guys rarely get many people looking out for them."

She nodded. "I know. I often stop when I'm on my walks to see how they're doing. I help when I can, but sometimes, all they seem to want is a kind word and for someone to notice them. It can make their day."

"I bet it does. Do you live around here?" This was getting interesting. How had I missed this gorgeous woman on my previous visits home?

Those almond eyes narrowed a fraction. "I've lived here all my life."

Her tone suggested I should know that, but I still couldn't place that face. "Me, too. Well, I've been away for a while, but I'm moving back if everything pans out."

"Lucky town."

Was that a hint of sarcasm beneath the sweetness? "It sure is. Maybe you could show me around to make me see what I've been missing."

"Oh, no, that won't work. I'm too busy to do that." She adjusted her grip on the pram and gave the tinsel a tweak with her gloved hand.

"Busy with your baby? How old?"

She bit her bottom lip, drawing my attention back to that full mouth. "Nine, twelve, and fifteen."

My eyebrows shot up. She was way too young to have children that age. "I meant the baby in the pram."

She lifted one shoulder, a defiant tilt to her chin. "They're all my babies, no matter how old they are."

I leaned closer and peered through the mesh netting. Three pairs of brilliant green eyes blinked back at me.

I jerked away, almost falling as my legs hit the bag of gifts I'd dropped. "You've got cats in that pram!"

A shiver of a smile crossed her face. "They can't be outside when it's this cold." She rested a hand on top of the pram cover, as if gently warning me not to get too close.

"Why are you pushing around three cats?" I looked back in at the cats. They were snuggled on a soft gray blanket. They looked content.

She let out a soft huff, and it clouded around her in the chilly air. "They have particular needs. Animals need help as well as people. You help the homeless, and I help the cats."

"Oh! Sure. I like cats. Is there something wrong with them? Is that why they have to be in a pram?"

"The only thing that's wrong with them is the way people have treated them."

I lifted a hand, seeing the fire in her eyes. "I get it. Sometimes, people don't have the sense they were born with. They can't walk?"

The anger in her pretty eyes faded a fraction. "Ginger only has three legs. He lost one after being attacked by a dog. If he walks too much, his back leg is at risk of dislocation, which leaves him in agony. Fluffball has arthritis, so it's painful for her to walk, but she likes to get outside. And Donut has a brain injury, so he can't walk in a straight line. It's too risky to let him free roam."

I whistled out a note. "That's quite a commitment, taking on three cats with special needs."

"I have six. Three of the cats stay at home. They have a large outdoor run, so get plenty of fresh air and exercise."

Oh, boy! I'd just found myself a pretty, crazy cat lady. I was smart enough to know not to tangle with a woman and her cats, but this woman was drawing me in.

I needed to know more about her. "They must keep you busy."

"Which is why I don't have time to show you around town. If you'll excuse me, I need to get home. I can't have my babies getting cold." She pushed the pram in front of her, her gaze fixed forward, her chin up.

I grabbed the sack of gifts and left it with Pete, before hurrying to catch up and walk beside her.

There was something special about this cat lady. Maybe it was the fire in her belly or her fierce protectiveness over something she loved. And her cute face was an added bonus.

She shot me a cautious glance as I caught up with her. "Are you going my way?"

"I need to grab something from my car. It's just up ahead. If you don't mind, I'll walk with you."

She gave another little shrug.

I couldn't resist sneaking a few glances at her as we walked. Those apple cheeks, wide mouth, and big dark eyes made her physically my type. But I wasn't just interested in looks. Sure, being attracted to your other half was important, but I needed to know the woman I was with was honest and straightforward. I'd been played around with before, and there was no way it was happening again.

She cleared her throat. "Um... what brings you back to Silver Birch?"

"Oh, you know, life. Things changing. New beginnings." I waved a hand in the air, not quite ready to lay everything out for her just yet. We all had pasts. Some of them messier than others.

"Well, welcome home. I'd never want to live anywhere else. I love it here."

"Small town life sure takes some beating. Do you have family here?"

"Don't we all?"

That wasn't an answer, more a side-step. "Sure. I mean, do your parents live around here?"

"Where's your car?"

"It's right there." I pointed at my new sleek black Audi, but I hadn't missed her avoiding my question again. Maybe she didn't get along with her parents. After all, you couldn't pick the family you were born into. There may be problems she didn't like to talk about. But I'd circle back to that when I got a moment.

And I planned to have more moments with this gorgeous woman. "Hey, you never told me your name."

She stopped the pink pram beside my car. Our gazes locked, and my pulse raced. She was a shot of sugar straight in the veins, making me feel like smiling for no reason.

"Is that important?"

"It will be the next time I bump into you. I've already told you my name. It's Gabe. Gabe Blackwell. And you are..."

She gave a swift nod. "Rhyannon."

"Just Rhyannon, like the singer?"

"For now." Her gaze ran over my car.

I placed a protective hand on it, just as she'd done with her cats. I'd only bought the car last week. It was a treat after securing the contract to refit the old Brewer's office block downtown. That money would see me right for years, give me a chance to put down roots, and find a place to call my own.

And I wanted to do that with someone. Maybe even someone like Rhyannon if she opened up a little and let me learn more about her.

"Do you like the car?" I said.

"So long as whatever I drive gets me from A to B, that's all I care about." Her gaze swept over the car again. It looked like her judgment of my new ride wasn't positive.

"Cars aren't for everyone. What kind of things do you like to do in your spare time?" I wanted to see what we had in common, and help bring down those walls Rhyannon had up.

Her fingers flexed around the pram handles. "I need to get these little ones inside and in the warm. We'll be late for their dinner if I don't hurry."

That was another side-step. Why all the mystery? "You're a real Christmas angel to unwanted cats."

A brief smile revealed two cute dimples, and my heart stuttered a beat.

"You could be too if you wanted to be. Unwanted animals always need protecting."

"I could. And I love animals. But how would that work?"

Rhyannon fumbled in her purse and handed me a card. "Meet me here tomorrow evening at six o'clock. That's where the Christmas magic happens for the cats."

I stared at the card. Forever Paws animal shelter. That name was familiar. I'd seen that somewhere before.

I lifted my head as she walked away. "Wait! Do you need a ride anywhere?"

"No, I've not got far to go." She glanced over her shoulder. "And don't you have elf duties to deal with?"

I cast a regretful look at the bag of gifts I'd left with Pete. I couldn't abandon what I was doing, no matter how cute this woman was. "What will we be doing at Forever Paws?"

"Helping those who need it the most, just as you do for the homeless. Enjoy your evening, Mr. Blackwell."

I would. I got satisfaction from giving back. And I also enjoyed watching Rhyannon walk away. I loved a curvy woman. And this one had fire in her as well as sweet dimples.

I looked back at the card and my grin widened. Had she just asked me out, or was this business?

I pulled out my phone and called Chris. "Guess what, buddy. I've found another mission that needs my attention. This one comes covered in fur."

There was something about this woman that intrigued me. And with some Christmas luck, I'd figure out just how amazing she was.

Chapter 2

♥

Rhyannon

I wasn't sure how I'd made it home, my knees were shaking so badly. And my heart raced as if I'd spotted an out-of-control freight train heading toward me, and I was stuck on the rails with my foot trapped in a hole.

After all this time, Gabe Blackwell was coming home. Possibly. The details were still wooly in my head. In fact, my whole head felt full of wool. I couldn't focus.

I unlocked my front door and carefully bumped the pram inside. I pulled off my thick winter gloves, frowning at the slight shake in my fingers.

"Get a grip of yourself. It's just Gabe."

Just Gabe! He was my ultimate high school crush. The gorgeous football player who stole so many hearts with his easy smile and broad shoulders. And now he was a gorgeous grown man who clearly had no idea who I was, even though I'd tutored him in science, so he didn't flunk out and lose his scholarship.

"Meow?"

"Oh! Sorry, sweetie. Mommy's just having a minor meltdown in the teenage crush department." I unzipped the pram cover, lifted Ginger out, scooped out Fluffball and gave her a quick tickle, and then extracted Donut.

Although I always promised the cats I didn't have a favorite, and I did love them all, Donut was my best furry baby. His past broke my heart, and I'd promised him he'd never be hurt again.

I snuggled him against me, stroking my fingers through his thick gray fur. "Did you enjoy your walk? It wasn't too cold for you?"

His loud purr rumbled through my chest and his paws kneaded the thick padding of my coat. He was always so happy. Despite everything he'd been through, he still loved and trusted people.

A chorus of meows greeted me as I walked through the house, Donut still in my arms. Sometimes, it was easier to carry him because he tended to walk in a circle due to his head trauma. It was an injury he almost didn't survive.

"I'm home, darling." I chuckled. There was no guy here to share all the fun I had with my cats. No one to ask about my day and cook me dinner.

I looked around at the scattering of cat toys and empty food bowls. What guy would put up with being last in line to a bundle of fluffy, demanding angels? Not a single one. I'd learned that the hard way.

The chorus of meows intensified, and three black cats appeared. Tom was missing an eye, Sinbad had no tail and a limp, and my final bundle of furry love,

Jolene, had no teeth, and needed her food mashed into tiny pieces so she could eat.

They may be imperfect and unlovable to many people, but this was my extended, amazing family, and I loved each and every one of them. They had my heart. They were welcome to it. The joy they gave me was bliss.

I was greeted with heads to rub and tails weaving around my legs as I sorted out six bowls and began dinner prep. This was never straightforward. Several of the cats were on medication, and sometimes giving them their pills felt like an Olympic sport. I usually succeeded by crushing the pills and covering them in tuna, or wrapping them in ham.

I shook my head. Gabe Blackwell was back. And boy, had he grown up from being an adorably cute boy who had no clue about science, to an out of this world hot full-grown man.

"Someone jab me with a claw. This can't be real."

I got several curious sounding meows in response.

"And what did I do? I invited him to Forever Paws tomorrow." I pointed a finger at the cats. "I blame you. You make me do silly things in the name of love."

The cats blinked at me, their focus on the food bowls.

After I'd administered the medicine, I placed down the bowls, and my gaggle of furry sweeties attacked.

I stepped away and switched on the kettle, before shrugging off my coat and taking off my winter boots and hat.

I made a mug of coffee and sipped it while I watched the cats eat. There was something so satisfying about making sure they were happy.

"You know, he dated Cassie for a couple of months while we were in school." I'd always hid my lion-sized crush on Gabe. It was uncool to crush on your friend's guy.

Donut glanced up at me, as if he was listening to me talk to myself.

I smiled at him. "They didn't last. And he let her down gently. Better than most guys did back then. Probably better than most guys would do now."

He blinked at me slowly and then returned to his food.

Donut was such a beautiful cat. When he'd arrived at Forever Paws, he'd been thin, his fur so matted it had to be shaved off, and he had an open wound on his head.

The second I'd seen him, I knew he had to come home with me. An animal who was so badly mistreated deserved a perfect home full of unconditional love, regardless of how many circles he walked in, or how long it took him to heal.

His medication was helping with his balance problems, but some days, the sweet little guy was unable to walk a straight line for all the tuna in the Pacific Ocean.

I held the warm mug close to my chest. "Now, you have competition in the gorgeous stakes. And Gabe also gives to the homeless. Could he be any more perfect? Handsome, sweet, and charitable."

I sighed, my sights landing on the cookie jar full of chocolate chip treats. Who was I kidding? The perfect guys never looked my way. I'd gotten used to being no-one's special lady.

I patted my soft belly, removing a few cat furs as I did so. A sweet tooth and an obsession with cats wouldn't catch Gabe's eye. And the second any guy realized I was a single woman with cats, they freaked out and ghosted me like I had the plague.

It was a dumb guy rule. A single female with cats was automatically seen as a nightmare.

Why couldn't they see it meant I had a big heart and just wanted all animals to have a good life?

Donut made his wobbly way over to me once he'd finished his food, taking his time as he staggered in several large circles.

My heart ached as he struggled, but the vet said he needed to practice his walking and I wasn't to coddle him. With time and medication, his balance should get better.

But how long should this go on? Was he suffering? Cats hid their physical pain so well. It had been three months, and Donut wasn't making any big improvements.

I set my mug down, crouched, and held my hands out to him. "You're almost there. You've made it this far. And you can spend the rest of the evening snuggled on my lap once you've had a go at walking straight. Come on, sweetie. You can do this."

My lap was prime real estate as far as the cats were concerned. Sometimes, three squeezed on at once, and there was often a fair amount of jostling as they got their places. It was a good job I had a generous lap for them to enjoy.

Donut's gaze fixed on mine and he did a slow blink. It was a show of his love for me.

I blinked right back. "You've got my heart. You all have."

Being around cats gave my heart a squeeze of pure joy. They all had their quirky personalities, likes and dislikes, and made friends and enemies, just like humans.

And I could always rely on them to be around, not minding what I wore and how long I wanted to stay curled up on the couch reading my latest novel. They accepted me, unlike a lot of people.

I'd heard the gossip about me being a spinster. It sounded like such a cold, sharp word. You had to hiss to say it.

Donut finally reached my outstretched fingers. He'd purred the whole time he was walking toward me, refusing to give up, despite how hard it must be for him or how dizzy he got. He never gave up when he wanted something. It was a life lesson to live by.

I scooped him into my arms and snuggled him against my chest. "You're such a clever boy. We'll soon have you back on your paws, then you won't need to go out in the pram anymore."

He butted my chin with the top of his head and the purring grew louder.

"When everyone is ready, let's head to the couch." I walked into the open plan lounge and set Donut on the couch. "Wait right there, I need to get my laptop." It was always risky having the laptop around the cats. They liked to lean against the fan and soak up its warmth, and the thing was forever overheating or getting clogged with fur.

But I needed to work on the finishing touches for the fundraiser for Forever Paws.

I stopped and brushed my fingers across the framed photograph on the mantle, showing me standing with my parents. They'd been gone almost two years, Mom to cancer and Dad six months after that. The doctor said he'd had a heart attack, but I was sure he'd died of a broken heart. He'd been lost without my mom by his side.

I looked around the lounge, a pulse of sadness radiating from my middle. I hadn't changed a thing in this house since they'd died.

Some people considered it creepy and added to my Miss Havisham vibe, having a mausoleum to my dead parents, but this was my home. And it had been their home. The photos, furniture, and ornaments reminded me of them. Why change anything?

I tilted my head and pursed my lips. I didn't love all the chintz, but I couldn't toss it out. And all those porcelain dolls held memories. I'd bought Mom most of them for her birthdays. Although some had mean little faces I wasn't too keen on.

I swallowed to remove the tightness in my throat. There was a happy outcome to having this big old place. I could fill it with cats. It was the sensible option. And I hadn't regretted a single second.

Besides, it wasn't as if I had an amazing husband wanting to give me half a dozen children to fill the bedrooms. Even if I did, I'd still have room for the cats.

"Meow?" Ginger twirled around my legs, never slowing down, despite missing a leg.

"You caught me dawdling again. I'm supposed to be working, aren't I?" I gathered up a notepad, my laptop, and some pens and headed back to the couch.

Fluffball and Jolene were settled on the end seat, snuggled together like the best buddies they were.

I settled next to them.

Donut was waiting to pounce. He leaped onto my lap, pressing his head against me, before kneading my legs.

The rest of my furry buddies took a few minutes to pick their favorite spots and settle in.

I set up the small laptop desk over Donut's head. It was risky. If he hopped up suddenly, everything would go flying, but it was the only way I could work with a cat on my lap.

I opened the file I'd been working on for the last few months and blew out a breath. "Fifty thousand needed to pay for the new heating. We have to make sure all your friends in the shelter don't get chilly this winter."

I got an ear flick and a tail twitch from a couple of the cats, but everyone looked like they were bedded down for the night.

Forever Paws had an ancient, groaning heating system straight out of the dark ages. It truly was a miracle it hadn't broken down yet. When it did, it would be a disaster.

My gaze went to the picture of me in my graduation gown, standing with my parents. School hadn't been the easiest of times for me, and I hadn't run with the cool gang.

Unlike Gabe. He'd been so cool, but not a total jerk. He'd had his moments of jerkiness. Teenage boys could be self-obsessed narcissists. But then, so could teenage girls. And I'd tangled with a few of them. Back then, I loved books, science, and board games. That didn't make me in line for prom queen. More like chess queen.

I tipped my head back and stared at the ceiling. I'd only asked Gabe to come to Forever Paws on the spur of the moment. We needed all the help we could get. Otherwise, I wouldn't have dared asked him.

I gently tickled Donut's chin. "I'd do anything for you lot. Even speak to my high school crush and figure out a way to get a donation from him."

And Gabe had money. I wasn't mercenary, but I was getting desperate to help the charity. He had to have spare money if he was driving such an expensive car. "Think of all the tins of cat food we could get with that car. Maybe even put down a big deposit on the heating so the contractor can start right after Christmas."

Donut simply squeezed his eyes shut and snuggled his nose into his tail.

"Let's hope that tomorrow, Gabe is feeling generous when he meets everyone at Forever Paws. That's if he even shows up."

I had a nervous, excited feeling in my stomach after bumping into Gabe. He may not remember me, but that wasn't important. He would help the cats. That's all that mattered. My fur babies came first.

Chapter 3

♥

Donut

Rhyannon's voice always gave me a little tingle of excitement. She spoke so softly and had such a calm tone that I sometimes fell asleep listening to her talk.

I often had no idea what she was talking about. Although she often talked about other cats, and I tried so hard not to be jealous. Rhyannon had a big heart and room for us all. And so long as I got lots of snuggles from her, I didn't mind too much.

Kindness ran through Rhyannon like a fine vintage of double cream.

I still remember the first time I saw her. Best day ever.

I'd gotten myself in a mess and was unable to stand up for long without needing to rest and sleep. Every time I moved, I felt sick.

I'd found a safe space at the back of my previous owner's bed. It hadn't been easy to get there. There were piles of clothes, smelly tissues, and old food boxes jammed under the bed. But I'd wriggled my way in and decided to stay there until I felt better.

I wasn't certain what happened next. There'd been banging and shouting and stamping feet. I must have gone to sleep for a while, but the next thing I remember, there was a light shining in my eyes and a strong smell of something antiseptic.

I snuggled against Rhyannon's soft sweater and let out a sigh. Every time I felt anxious about what I'd been through, I only had to see her and I felt a hundred times better.

Before I moved here, Rhyannon spent hours talking to me, sitting next to my pen at Forever Paws and encouraging me out.

I saw tears on her cheeks several times, but couldn't figure out why she was so sad. But I just knew she was kind. She was soft, patient, and thoughtful, always bringing me little treats and always saying sorry when she startled me.

The first time I let her hold me, she cried until those tears fell on what was left of my fur, which hadn't been much back then. And those strange little human tears that dampened my fur did something to me.

I'd been so full of fear and pain that I'd wanted to close my eyes and never wake up. But those tears took away the scary feelings. Not all of them, but they eased, and they kept on easing. One day, I reckon they'll be gone.

Rhyannon had opened her arms and her home to me, even though I walk funny.

That's not to say I still don't let my old fears get to me. I'm suspicious of those pills she sneaks into my food, even when that food is delicious, pungent tuna, but I feel better after taking them. I wobble less.

And it wasn't easy when I first arrived. I had trials to get through. We have a hierarchy in this house, and it keeps changing. I wasn't fighting for top position, not with my balance issues, but I know when I'm strong and fit again, I'll stake my claim.

Even now, one of the other cats can get spiteful and swipe at me, but we all have our issues to deal with, and most of the time, we get on okay. And so long as I get a regular snuggle with Rhyannon, I'm happy.

I wouldn't change anything about this place. Rhyannon is so soft and soothing. I love nothing more than lying on her lap. It helps me forget the other place, the pain I felt, and how hungry I'd get. I used to dream about plates of chicken. I've heard humans say animals don't dream. You should try living in my dreams of chicken, tuna, and warm plates of gravy. I could drool just thinking about it.

Before Rhyannon, I'd spend a lot of time on my own, just like she does now. I'd hide from the two big dogs I lived with. I could tell from the look in their dumb doggy eyes that they considered me a plaything or a meal, especially when our owner forgot to feed us.

I even got a nasty nip on my tail from one of them. That taught me to stay well away.

And then there were the children. There'd been five little humans, and they weren't always gentle with me.

I never hurt them, no matter how hard they tugged on my fur, and not even when one of the little ones pulled a whole handful out. But it was easier to be on my own when I lived there.

Maybe something like that happened to Rhyannon. She preferred her own company because her hair got pulled and someone bit her.

I've never bitten Rhyannon. I never would. I love her.

I'd always thought she was happy being with us. But recently, I've heard her crying in bed. And she watches a lot of what I now know are called rom-coms. I bet we'll watch one later when she's finished her work.

And she always sighs when watching those movies. She says real life isn't like that, and there's no such thing as a perfect guy.

I have no clue if that's true. But maybe if she finds a nice guy, that'll stop her crying. She needs to find someone to make her smile all the time. She smiles now, sometimes, but it always looks a bit sad to me.

And I know sadness. I hate Rhyannon being sad.

I'm making it my mission to find this man. Someone who likes snuggles and wears big, warm sweaters I can sleep on.

Fluffball rolled onto her side, stretched, and hopped off the couch. She sidled to the door and glanced over her shoulder, looking at me with her big yellow eyes.

I stared back at her and blinked. What did she want?

She jerked her head toward the corridor and then disappeared.

Uh, oh! I recognized that gesture. It meant we needed to talk, so you'd better come find me or I'll whack you over the head with a paw. Fluffball may look like a cutie, but she could be mean.

After a moment, the rest of the cats also sidled out of the room. They must also have spotted the signal to regroup for a private meeting. No humans allowed.

Nerves tickled my belly. And not in a fun, human finger kind of way. I had the toughest job on my paws, sneaking out without Rhyannon noticing me.

I tried to slide off her knees, but she caught me and gave a gentle laugh.

"You're leaving me, too? Anyone would think you're off to have a secret meeting you don't want me to overhear." She kissed the top of my head, before setting me on the floor. "Off you go. Go play with the others."

I wobbled out of the lounge, trying to play it cool, and managed to do only one circle before I got into the corridor and started my search for the other cats.

Whatever was going on, I had to be involved, especially if it had to do with Rhyannon. She'd kept me safe and given me a second chance, so I'd keep her safe, too.

Even if I had to fight Fluffball to do it.

Chapter 4

Gabe

I swung my arms as I stood outside the entrance of the Forever Paws animal shelter, waiting for Rhyannon to show. It was ice city around here, too cold to snow, but it would fall again once the temperature rose a few degrees.

Despite the frigid surroundings, my insides felt warm at the prospect of seeing Rhyannon again.

I was certain I'd met her before, and tonight I'd find out where this gorgeous woman fit into my life, and how I could keep her around.

"Hi, there. May I help you with something?" A middle-aged woman with bright eyes, wearing a sweater with a large cat's face on, peered out the main door.

"Hey. I'm waiting for someone. She volunteers here. Rhyannon."

The woman's eyes twinkled. "I'm sure she'll be along soon. She never lets the cats down. Come inside, you don't want to freeze while you wait."

I took a quick glance back at the parking lot and then headed inside, grateful for the welcoming warmth that hit me. "Wow! You go all out for Christmas. Are the cats appreciating your efforts?" The place looked like Santa's elves had thrown a giant tinsel party.

The woman gave a tinkling laugh. "I'm certain some of them do. I'm Mulberry. I volunteer here, the same as Rhyannon."

"Good to meet you, Mulberry. I'm Gabe. A... friend of Rhyannon's." And a whole lot more if she'd let me get to know her better.

"It's great to meet one of her friends. Rhyannon works so hard. She's always going out of her way to help. I couldn't wish for a more wonderful volunteer, especially at this time of year. Everyone gets caught up in organizing Christmas and having big family gatherings. I understand how important that is, but the cats can get over-looked when people have so many things to get done."

My heart stuttered. I hadn't even thought that Rhyannon was unavailable. She may already be married. "Does Rhyannon have a big family?"

Mulberry patted my arm. "I'm sure she will one day. Come and see our Christmas wonderland. And I can't let you leave until you've had a look at our Wall of Joy."

I was happy to accept a mug of hot chocolate as Mulberry led me around and regaled me with tales of happy endings for the furry residents. Everywhere was covered in Christmas cards, sparkling lights, and decorations.

I stopped in front of a huge wall covered in photographs of owners and their cats. "This is the wall you mentioned?"

"That's right. Isn't it something?" Mulberry said. "I love to hear from the people who found their perfect cat. We often get cards and letters from adopters, telling us about their wonderful cats. Cats always make life better. Don't you think?"

"You won't hear me disagreeing."

"Do you have any cats?"

"No, but I'm just making the move back to Silver Birch. I need to get settled before I think about making new additions to the family."

"When you are settled, you must come for another visit. I'm certain I will find you your perfect cat. There's a cat for everyone. It's just a case of matchmaking them."

"It sounds like you'll set me up on a date."

"I expect you'll have plenty of opportunities to go on dates as well," Mulberry said. "And a handsome man like you won't be troubled for a lack of company. I can picture you with a special lady. Someone with a kind heart."

I chuckled. "I hope that's true. And I know what I'm looking for."

"It's good when a man knows his own mind. It saves on a lot of misunderstanding." She pointed to a picture. "I'm particularly fond of this couple."

A petite, elfin-faced woman stood with a tall guy who had his arm wrapped around her waist. Lounging over the woman's shoulder was a stunning, long-haired Siamese cat with the most incredible blue eyes.

"They adopted that cat from here?" I asked.

"That's right. And not only did this lady find a long-lost cat who meant the world to her, she was also reunited with someone from her past. They're getting married soon, and I've got an invitation to the wedding."

"Wow! Imagine that. Adopt a cat and get a free husband."

Mulberry laughed and patted my arm again. "I can't wait. I love a wedding. I take it you aren't married if you're planning on finding a special lady."

I grinned to myself. She sure was nosy, but it was done in a friendly way, so I couldn't object. "Not yet."

The door behind us opened. I turned, my emotions flaring as Rhyannon hurried in, pushing the pink pram in front of her.

Her eyes widened as they settled on me, and a charming flush crossed her cheeks. "Oh! You came. I... I wasn't sure you would. The weather's been terrible."

"Of course, I came. I'd never turn down an invitation from a beautiful woman with such pretty cats."

Mulberry softly hummed a note of approval.

Rhyannon ducked her head and fussed with the pram cover. "I thought you might still be busy giving out gifts to the homeless."

"Oh! You help the homeless?" Mulberry asked. "What a wonderful thing to do."

"Everyone needs a little extra help at this time of year," I said, my focus on Rhyannon, who'd yet to meet my gaze for more than half a second. She was so adorable the way she got flustered over a compliment.

Rhyannon unzipped the pram cover, and the head of a sleek fluffy gray cat poked out.

"Who is this?" I walked over and held my hand out to the cat.

It sniffed me tentatively a few times and then glanced up at Rhyannon as if seeking her reassurance.

"This is Donut," she said. "Donut, I'd like you to meet Gabe."

"Hey, buddy. How you doing?" I gently tickled the cat's head. "How'd he get that big scar on the back of his head?"

Rhyannon glanced at Mulberry, who was busy shuffling paper around on the reception desk, and looking like she was trying not to listen in. "We're not sure. He arrived with several horrible injuries. They affect his balance. Donut has trouble walking in a straight line."

"Is that how you got your name?"

The cat purred, a powerful rumble deep in his chest.

"That's amazing. Donut's not normally friendly with strangers. He gets easily scared." Rhyannon pulled off her green fluffy hat, and her blonde hair floated around her head.

As I looked up at her, the sense I already knew her intensified. "We have met before, haven't we?"

She arched an eyebrow, and a sparkle of amusement lit her gaze. "We have. I wondered if you'd figure it out."

I stood from petting Donut. My gaze ran over Rhyannon, taking in her cute nose, big eyes, and smile. "I just can't put my finger on it. We didn't date?" I was certain I'd remember someone so sweet.

She huffed out a breath. "No, we never dated. But does the name Cassie Montgomery mean anything to you?"

"Sure. From school? You know Cassie?"

"I do. I'm her best friend. Rhyannon Sitterly."

I took a step back, and my hand landed over my heart. "How did I not recognize you? You made sure I aced science. Well, you helped me get a solid C, so I didn't lose my scholarship." Had she always been this cute?

"That's right. And I've changed a bit since school. I've gotten rid of the braces and figured out how to tame my hair."

"You were in the chess club?"

Her cheeks flushed. "You remember that about me?"

"Of course. I never could get my head around that game. I wanted to learn, though."

She pursed that pretty mouth of hers. "Sure you did. You were too busy racing around a muddy field to learn chess."

I tilted my head. "Maybe I'd have liked to play chess, but wasn't brave enough to go into a room full of super brains, like you."

I couldn't help but laugh as her jaw dropped.

"You're kidding?"

"Kind of. Although I was all about football and hanging out with the guys back then. Maybe now, you could show me how to play."

She lifted a shoulder, a small smile on her face. "Maybe I will."

"How's Cassie doing? I lost touch with her ages ago."

"She's great. We're still close. She lives around here. She got married a year ago, and works in the local pharmacy."

Donut slid out of the cat pram and wobbled his way to my legs.

I ducked down again and petted him. The cat made short work of climbing onto my knees and pressing against my chest.

"He's really something. You're a gorgeous cat." I glanced up at Rhyannon. "Are you okay?" Her eyes looked misty, as if she was about to cry.

She blinked and looked away. "Of course."

Mulberry walked over, a sleek tabby cat in her arms. "I need to make a few calls in the back office. They could take a while. I'll leave the two of you to go over the plans for the fundraiser."

"Is there anything I can help with?" Rhyannon asked.

Mulberry shook her head and glanced my way. "No, you stay here with Gabe and sort things out." She smiled at me, before turning and leaving the room.

A grin spread across my face. This meant I got to spend time alone with Rhyannon. And although we were just reconnecting, I had a feeling I'd enjoy spending time getting to know her. This evening couldn't have gone better.

"Let me take Donut from you," Rhyannon said. "You'll get covered in fur."

"I can handle a bit of fur." I stood and lifted the cat onto my shoulder. He draped himself there like it was his favorite place.

"He really seems to like you," Rhyannon said. "He's only ever like that with me."

"And I like him. It hurts my heart to think that someone mistreated him." I stroked a hand down his soft back.

A flash of pain crossed Rhyannon's face. "I don't understand how anyone could do that. These animals need our love and protection, not mistreatment. All they want is a chance at a happy home and for someone to love them."

My throat tightened at the sadness in her voice.

"That's why I help out at Forever Paws whenever I can. When I heard they needed money for a new heating system, I volunteered to get the funding."

Oh, jeez. She had a heart of gold and the face of an angel. "You really are an angel to these cats."

Rhyannon smiled. "I do what I can to help."

"And I want to help, too."

Her face brightened. "You do? I hoped you'd say that. We're always looking for donations."

"I'll donate. But I also want to help raise the rest of the money. Do you need any more volunteers for that?"

"Always!"

"Then it's sorted. And since it sounds like you don't get much free time, we can combine fundraising plans with dinner."

A cute little snort shot out of her. "You're... asking me out to dinner?"

"Sure. We should catch up. I expect a lot's gone on with you since school. I want to know everything. And I've lost touch with a lot of the old crowd." I should never have lost touch with this sweet woman, but in high school, I was a football-obsessed goon.

Several long beats of my heart filled the silence. Was Rhyannon going to turn me down and was scrambling for an excuse to say no gently?

"Only if you want to," I said. "I'm not—"

"I definitely do want dinner. That would be great." The words flew from her lips. "But not much has changed in my life. You might be bored."

"I know a few things must have changed." I hesitated. "Are you seeing someone? You're not free to date?"

"No! Definitely not. I'm one hundred percent single. I spend all my spare time here."

How could such a catch not have gotten scooped up years ago? The guys around here must be idiots. "Then name the place. I'll take you there right away."

Rhyannon's eyes sparkled, but she shook her head. "Not tonight. And I have a better idea. Let me show you around Forever Paws. I want you to fall in love with the place as much as I have. These cats will capture your heart."

I grinned as I handed her back Donut. "Whatever you want." So long as I got to spend more time with Rhyannon, I was happy.

Chapter 5

♥

Rhyannon

"This is Cat Alley." My heart was a racing ball of tangled emotions as I continued to show Gabe around Forever Paws. It still amazed me that he hadn't turned down the offer of a tour.

This guy needed to do something wrong, because he was quickly falling into my perfect guy category. And that meant he was way out of my league.

"It's a great setup you've got here." Gabe strolled along beside me. He'd been sweet, a little flirty, and kind all evening. Plus, his good looks had my insides flipping. And if that wasn't enough, he didn't mind one bit that he had several of Donut's furs still plastered to him. A guy who loved cats was total swoon city.

"They do amazing work here. The cats brought to the shelter are often in terrible condition. But with the right medical care, love, and devotion, they make a full recovery and we find them their perfect homes. It can take time to find the right match, though."

"The perfect match is always worth waiting for." He winked at me. "And once I find myself a permanent place, I'm thinking about getting a cat."

Oh, sweet mercy. He was throwing out those comments and making my heart pound. Those words were like catnip to me. I managed an affirmative sounding noise.

"Mulberry suggested it. I think she'd have picked a cat out for me right away if I'd said yes to taking one home."

I laughed, trying to sound light-hearted. A man who liked cats was another tick in the perfect guy box. "Mulberry can be a bit pushy, but her heart is in the right place. Just like me, she wants to see all our cats find their forever homes."

"We all need one of those."

"Let me show you the rehab room. Then there's the clinic and maternity room."

"Maternity room?"

"We often get pregnant mamas in who need a little extra care and attention. And then we get the abandoned kittens to look after. Bottle feeding them is the best." I grinned at him.

"It sounds great. Lead the way."

"Last year, we re-homed almost a thousand cats, performed two hundred and fifty operations, completed almost six hundred home checks for people looking for cats, and went through over five thousand tins of cat food." I glanced at him. There was a huge grin on his face. "What's so funny?"

"Nothing. I love your enthusiasm. It shows you care."

My heart thundered. Everything Gabe did made me tingle. He loved cats, he was funny, he made my toes curl, and I'd only been around him a couple of days. Imagine how I'd feel if we went to dinner together and it kept going so well?

I needed to get a grip. This was just my old feelings making me revert to geek girl teenage crush overload. They'd pass. They had to. Because if they didn't, I was in a whole heap of trouble.

No, this wasn't real. I was simply surprised about meeting Gabe after all this time. I wasn't into him. We'd both grown up and changed.

But he'd changed for the better.

The touch of his hand on my arm sent a shiver down to my toes and up to my heart. "Hey, I wasn't teasing you. I admire what you do. I'm glad you invited me to see Forever Paws, Rhyannon. And I definitely want to help."

I could hear my name on his lips all day, every day. "Um, that's great. You really do?"

"Of course. How much do you need to raise?"

"Fifty thousand."

He whistled through his teeth. "That's a big chunk of change. How much have you raised so far?"

"About fifteen thousand. We've held a few fundraisers and a raffle, but it's hard to get people to part with their money at this time of year. Christmas is an expensive time, especially if you have a family to buy gifts for. I know people give what they can, but I'm worried we won't reach the target. We've got a contractor who can do the work after Christmas, but he's pressing for a deposit. If we're not quick, he'll take on another job."

"Slow down. We've got this." Gabe placed his large, warm hands on my shoulders and turned me toward him. "We can do this. You just have to get people to see how amazing this place is."

My stupid heart felt like it turned to mush as I stared into his eyes and then looked at his mouth. This wasn't flirting. Gabe was being nice. He was reassuring me that we'd raise the money.

But if this wasn't flirting, why was my heart racing like a speeding train running late to pick up the president?

"You know, I always think better on a full stomach," he said. "How about that dinner?"

As if my own stomach heard those words, it grumbled.

He laughed, shooting me a heart-stopping smile. "It sounds like you need food as well. And I'd really like to take you out."

Was this a dream? I was about to wake, covered in cats, drooling on my pillow, having never met Gabe again.

"Hey, is something wrong?" he said.

"No! Everything's great. Just perfect."

"So... are you going to break my heart and turn me down?"

Me? Turn him down? "I don't..." remember how to speak? Know how to form a sentence? Forgot how to say the word yes?

"What do you say, Rhyannon Sitterly? Will you go out with me?"

Dear Lord, this was a date. I had to play it cool and not blow it. "Sure. But not tonight. I've got to finalize the details for the fundraiser. I can't let myself get distracted."

"Cats before dudes. Got it. I respect that."

Gabe got it, and he hadn't run away laughing at the crazy cat lady. He was officially perfect.

"You will go out with me, though?" he said.

"Yes. I will."

He stepped closer, and the air in the room seemed to vanish. "Tomorrow night?"

"Uh, huh. Yup." I nodded vigorously to show I was happy. More than happy. I wanted to dance along Cat Alley and tell the cats I'd just been asked out by the gorgeous Gabe Blackwell.

His wide grin almost dazzled me, and those lips were getting dangerously close to mine.

I couldn't do anything but stare at him.

"I'll pick you up at seven. Where do you live?" he asked.

"Oh! In the same place. I haven't moved."

"You still live with your folks on Broad Lane?"

"I'm in the same house. Do you remember where it is?"

"Of course." The smile stayed on his face, only tempting me to inch closer. "I'll come get you."

"I can meet you at the diner, or wherever we're going. I don't want you to go to any trouble."

His hand brushed down my arm, making my heart spasm. "Absolutely not. We're doing this date properly. I'll pick you up."

All I could do was nod and smile and try not to stumble over my own feet as I continued to show him around. I had a date with Gabe Blackwell. Best gift ever.

Chapter 6

Donut

I yawned, taking a few seconds to do a full body stretch, arching my back and then rolling over to push my paws to the sky. I called the move an upward facing cat. I deserved this. Yesterday had gone perfectly.

After my conversation with the others, we'd agreed Rhyannon needed a guy in her life. We hadn't figured out exactly how we'd find that guy, but the motion was passed. And after my trip to Forever Paws last night, everything clicked into place.

It had taken some persuasion to get everyone on board to begin with. Fluffball had led the meeting. Being female, she often had sensible ideas, and I always listened to her.

She insisted Rhyannon was lonely, and although we helped fill the empty space in her heart, she needed something else. Something only a guy could give her. I wasn't sure what that was, but apparently it involved kissing and snuggles in bed when we weren't allowed to watch. I was still in two minds about that. I liked to share a pillow with Rhyannon when she let me.

Ginger hadn't agreed with adding a human guy into the mix. He claimed he could provide Rhyannon with all the love she needed.

But Fluffball was adamant. And when she got snooty and hissy, we all backed down. She was scary when she didn't get her own way.

After much debating and a fair few swipes from Fluffball, her claws extended, we were all in agreement.

I had my doubts about having a man around too often. From my experience, they were loud, often clumsy, and lost their keys and phone all the time. But they could also be useful when it came to fixing broken stuff and getting things off high shelves. Some of them, anyway.

Rhyannon was terrible at anything involving tools. She once drilled a hole through a pipe in the wall and flooded the basement when she attempted to put up shelves. She'd cried that day.

The problem was, she hated strangers coming into the house to repair things. And I was in full agreement with her over that. I hated the strange smells and noises other humans made. Strangers weren't for either of us. But that meant things got stuck on high shelves and broken things didn't get mended.

But I'd make an allowance about letting in a stranger if Rhyannon was lonely. It made me glum to hear her crying at night when she was alone. It would sometimes take me ages to stop her from crying. I'd have to use all my cute tricks, like laying on her head, biting her toes through the duvet, and rolling onto my back and flicking my tail in her face to make her laugh.

Eventually, she'd snuggle me close and tell me I was a goofball.

A goofball meant you were awesome, so I was happy about that.

If a noisy, loud man stopped those tears, then that's what needed to happen.

And when I'd discovered Gabe at Forever Paws, I got an excited tingle all down my back to the tip of my tail.

The second I heard his voice, I sensed his goodness. He had kind eyes and smiled a lot. Those were good signs to look out for. And I could spot a fake smile. It didn't reach the eyes and made the human look scary.

And Gabe was happy to snuggle me. It had taken all my courage to creep out of the cat pram and meet him. But I'd had to put him to the test. I needed to make sure he'd be good enough for Rhyannon.

I instantly knew those big strong hands would do the job. And I made sure to leave extra fur on his clothes. Anyone who didn't mind their love coming with a bit of fur would have a problem if they were in Rhyannon's life.

She vacuumed daily and was always racing around with a large broom sweeping up after us, but we still left a few furry presents dotted around.

Personally, I hated the vacuum. It was noisy. It roared at me and always seemed to be heading in my direction.

Sometimes, I got all twisted around trying to escape it, and Rhyannon would have to help me out.

But she didn't use the vacuum to be mean, only to keep the fur under control. I've always believed love was better when it came with fur.

Getting back to Gabe, I'd also checked his snuggle technique. It was reassuring. He'd gotten a nice hold on me, but not too tight, so I felt trapped. And when I made the move to squirm onto his shoulder, he'd laughed and helped me. He had great shoulders, and could probably sit all of us on them if he held out his arms.

I also took a careful note of the way he spoke to Rhyannon. Everything sounded positive, although some words got lost in translation. I have to concentrate hard since my head injury to make sense of all the human words.

But the way Rhyannon kept giggling and blushing, with not a tear in sight, suggested she liked him.

Keeping a firm hold on that knowledge, I'd snuggled back in my cat pram, happy to have it all to myself for a change.

When I got home, I'd raced around as quickly as my circular walk would allow, and gathered the others. I even had the cheek to disturb Fluffball as she came out of the litter box. That earned me a swipe of her paw, but I didn't mind. I had to tell them the news straightaway, before I got things muddled.

Everyone had approved. Gabe was the man for Rhyannon.

Now, it was time for phase two. We needed to figure out how to get Gabe to move in and make sure Rhyannon never cried again.

Chapter 7

♥

Rhyannon

It felt like tiny icicles were forming on my nose as I hunched behind the bush, being careful not to slide into the pile of snow behind me.

My phone vibrated, and I checked the message. *Any sign of our elusive furball?*

I replied to Cassie. *Nope. But he can't resist the tuna smell for much longer. Give it time.*

We've been out here an hour. I'm freezing my bits off.

15 more minutes. I'll treat you to hot chocolate afterward.

I got back a sad face and a mug of cocoa.

My reply was a cat face emoji. After all, we were here to help an injured feral cat. He'd be much colder than us, despite having a layer of fur. And it was freezing tonight. Even with a padded thermal coat on and three pairs of socks, I was shivering and my toes were numb.

We had to catch Turbo. That was the nickname Forever Paws had given the young tomcat who'd evaded all attempts to catch him.

He'd get to the cage set with tempting treats and then speed off like a bullet train before the door closed.

He had me worried. The last time he'd been seen, he had a bad limp. I was concerned a car had hit him and could have more serious injuries.

Turbo had to be caught before the cold or his injuries defeated him.

My phone vibrated again. *I see him!*

I inched my head around the bush, careful to stay low so as not to scare Turbo. My breath quickened. There he was, sniffing the side of the cage.

My throat tightened as I took in his appearance. One of his ears was torn, he had dried blood on his fur, and was dragging one back leg. This handsome cat was in trouble. We had to get him tonight, or it would be too late to save him.

I didn't move. Didn't even breathe. My eyes watered because I wasn't blinking as Turbo inched closer to the delicious tuna and soft bedding waiting for him.

Cats were so stubborn. It was a self-preservation response, but I wish he knew how desperately I wanted to help him, and how happy he'd be once his wounds were treated and he found his perfect home.

I clasped my hands together and wished for a miracle. Just a few more steps, and the door would shut.

Turbo hesitated, his ears low. Would his hunger overcome his wariness this time and he'd step inside?

The cat looked around, then leaned into the cage. He couldn't get to the food until he was all the way in. There was no option for him to grab and run. Although I doubted he'd be able to run anywhere with that leg in such poor shape.

His whiskers were stiff and his little nose wrinkling as he sniffed the air.

Any second now, and he'd be safe.

Turbo stepped inside and limped toward the food. The door mechanism triggered, and it shut behind him. One feral cat safely caught.

As much as I wanted to whoop, I knew the procedure. Keep things calm and quiet. Cassie would do the same. We'd worked the evening cat rescue shift for years. Everything needed to be chilled or our capture would get even more anxious.

We emerged from our hiding places, grinning from ear to ear, and gave each other a quiet high five.

I bopped beside the cage. "Hello, handsome. You've seen some rough times by the look of you."

Turbo hissed, the tasty food beside him forgotten as his large eyes scanned for an escape route.

"Oh, baby, don't be mad," Cassie said softly, her voice muffled by her thick green scarf. "You're going to be so spoiled and pampered. We'll get that leg healed and a nice lap for you to curl up on."

I did a quick visual inspection of Turbo. He was skinny and grubby, but it was his leg I was most worried about. "Let's cover the cage and get him in the car. The sooner the vet looks him over the better."

Cassie produced a blanket, and we snuggled it around the cage. We hurried back to the car parked by the side of the road with the cage balanced between us.

Turbo howled for the whole two minutes it took us to transport him. This little guy was a fighter.

It wasn't until the cage stopped moving and was secured that he went quiet.

I peeked at him under the blanket and got another hiss for my troubles. "Let's get out of here."

"Straight to Forever Paws?" Cassie slid into the passenger's seat and buckled up.

"You got it. The vet's holding a late night surgery, so we should be able to get Turbo seen right away. Let's hope that back leg can be saved."

"Forever Paws is the place of miracles. If anyone can save him, it'll be our amazing charity."

We kept our voices low so as not to stress Turbo as we talked. He may not be used to being around people.

"I'm so glad we got him," I said. "He's like the invisible cat. I thought we'd never get him in that cage."

"Me too. He must have been on the streets for a while to get so good at hiding."

"He'll need a special home to give him time and plenty of love so he can learn to trust." I glanced at Cassie. "Have you got room for him?"

She grinned and shook her head. "I took in three abandoned kittens and a lame guinea pig just last night. Mulberry called me around midnight with an emergency intake. I couldn't say no."

I chuckled. Cassie was as animal mad as me. It's why we were such good friends. "And I don't have room. Plus, Turbo might be too feisty for my gang to handle."

"What we have back there hissing and growling at us is a guy's cat," Cassie said. "A strapping male cat needs a good strong role model."

"Sure he does. Once Turbo's had the snip, he won't be so feisty. He'll be happy with a nice, quiet little old lady to snuggle with."

"Don't listen to her Turbo. Mean old Rhyannon is joking about you getting the snip," Cassie whispered, nodding knowingly at me.

All the cats who came to Forever Paws were spayed and neutered. And the full toms always calmed down after their operation.

"I really think he needs a guy in his life," she said.

"I wonder if Gabe would be a good fit for him." I shot a glance at Cassie. I hadn't meant to say that out loud, but Gabe had been on my mind ever since we'd bumped into each other.

"Gabe who?"

"Um, Gabe from school. Do you remember him?"

"You mean, Gabe Blackwell!"

I kept my eyes on the road. "Yep. That's the one. Your old flame."

She snorted a laugh. "Oh, he's not an old flame. I mean about a hundred years ago in high school we dated a few times, but that was nothing serious. Is Gabe visiting for the holidays?"

"I'm not sure. He could be staying for longer." I licked my chapped lips. "I expect I'll find out more when we grab dinner together."

Cassie clutched my arm. "No, you don't! You don't drop a bomb like that and act like everything's normal. Gabe asked you out?"

I kept focused on the road. "It's just food. We'll be talking about the Forever Paws fundraiser. He may be able to help out." I glanced at Cassie. She had her laser-like stare fixed on me, and must be able to hear the lie in my voice.

"So... this dinner is just business?"

I nodded. "That's right. Don't distract me. It's icy on these roads, and we have precious cargo on board."

Turbo howled as if he knew he was being talked about.

"Don't worry, cutie pie. We'll have you safe and warm in no time," I said.

Cassie was quiet for a minute, and I was hopeful she'd change the subject. "I liked Gabe in high school. He was a half-decent guy to date. A bit full of himself, but he was a football player. They always got their egos massaged. You tutored him in science, didn't you?"

"Yep."

"And now he's..."

"Not sure. From his flash car, it must be something that pays well. Maybe finance. I don't know."

"Oh, come on! Stop playing it cool. I know you crushed on him when we were in school."

My cheeks heated. "You did? I mean, I don't remember. Maybe I did."

"Stop it! You're a terrible liar. You're also an excellent friend. And even though you blushed and twirled your hair every time he stopped by our lunch table, I trusted you a hundred percent not to make a move on my guy."

"As if that would have ever worked." I glanced at her. "Not that I'd ever make a move on Gabe, or any guy you like, just so we're clear."

Cassie laughed. "I know. And that's because you're awesome. It's why I love you."

I grinned. "There's that, but also because guys at school looked right through me."

"Hey, don't be so down on yourself. They only looked through you because you were scary smart. They didn't want their fragile reputations shattered when you called them out in class."

"I never did that."

"Only because you were too polite and didn't want to hurt their fragile male feelings."

Cassie had a point. I'd also kept my head down in class so I wouldn't draw attention to myself. No one likes a smart alec.

"My feelings aren't important. Gabe's moved on from those days. He's a success, and I'm still... me." I sighed. "I'm the same as I was back in high school. The same person he left behind to go make a name for himself. I mean, not left behind. It's not like I had a claim on him. But he's changed. I haven't."

"Your feelings?"

"Um, you know what I mean. My old crush feelings. I don't have them now." She could easily tell that was a lie.

"Huh! You don't say?"

I nodded. "How about we listen to some Christmas tunes?"

She swatted my hand away from the radio. "You have changed. You're different from school. And you stay here because you love this place. You have everything you need right here. Which includes me. You're not allowed to move away. I'd miss you too much."

"That's true. But I haven't changed much. I still cut my own hair, have way too many sweaters with cats on to be considered normal, and enjoy knitting comfort blankets for unloved kitties. I used to do all those things when I was seventeen."

"Your hair is cute, your sweaters are adorable, and the cats love those knitted things you churn out. They suck on them."

"Yeah, it helps to relieve their stress. But... I've stuck to the same mold, and Gabe is so... well, you should see him."

Cassie whacked my arm. "He can't be hotter than he was in school."

"Yep. At least ten times hotter."

She blew out a breath. "Having eye candy around is never a chore, but do you care about that? You had your teenage crush, but you don't still like him, do you?"

"I shouldn't bother liking him. It's a big old waste of time. I should get: warning, crazy cat lady tattooed on my forehead so I don't waste the guy's time."

Cassie eyed my forehead. "I'm not sure all those words would fit on such a small space. Maybe you could knit it on a sweater."

"I've already done that."

Cassie's chuckle died. "Rhyannon, you're smart and funny and care about other people. And don't get me started on what you do for those cats. And you do the best home haircuts. I wouldn't let you near me with scissors if you made me look like a scarecrow. Plus, you save me a fortune by not having to go to the salon and endure vacation small talk and get upsold over-priced shampoo."

"And I'm always happy to shear you." I glanced at the twinkling lights in the front yard of a large house as we drove past. "I don't know why it's bothering me that Gabe's back in town."

"Hmmm, I've got a good idea. Is it because you still like him?"

"I... maybe I do. Do you have a problem with that?"

She laughed. "Not for a second. Gabe was a fun boy to date, but I'm not going to slap you for going out with him. You're a free agent, and he's a free agent... wait, he is single?"

"Um, yeah. I mean, I think so. I didn't ask." What if this really was just business for Gabe?

It couldn't be, he'd been so flirty with me. But maybe he was being kind. I wanted to whack my head on the steering wheel. It was no surprise I stayed away from relationships when they made me act like this.

"Ask him! You have to make sure the playing field is clear, before you go in for the kill," Cassie said.

"I should stick to cats. They're so much simpler." I tensed at the sound of Turbo vomiting in his cage.

"Eek! Put your foot down. This little guy doesn't like car rides," Cassie said.

I sped up a fraction, still hyper aware of the poor conditions. What was that about cats being simpler? They were definitely messier with the fur, and hairballs, and litter trays. Well, messier than some guys. If things progressed with Gabe, would he put up with my cat obsession? He'd have to. I wasn't giving them up. Not ever.

I shook my head. I was getting way ahead of myself. One sort of date didn't mean a ring on my finger.

I shivered and grinned. Could this be the start of something new? My heart pounded at the possibility of a future with Gabe.

"You've got a sappy grin on your face," Cassie said. "You so want to date Gabe Blackwell."

"I want to explore the possibility."

She poked me with a finger. "Then do it. I'm thrilled for you. Just make sure he's good enough. And stop putting yourself down. You're a strong, confident, fur-covered, cat crazy proud woman. Viva la cats!"

I laughed along with Cassie. "Yes! Viva la cats!"

Chapter 8

Gabe

I waited outside the large black wrought-iron gates as they eased open, before pulling my Audi up to the front of Rhyannon's house.

I whistled out a high note as I took in the huge double-fronted detached building. I'd forgotten she lived in such an enormous place. I'd never been here when I was a kid, but knew where her family lived. Her dad used to run Silver Birch's largest realtor, and the family got wealthy by sharing their passion for living in a small town.

Rhyannon's parents must be retired by now. Maybe she was staying here to take care of them. It would be the sort of thing she'd do, making sure her family was looked after. This woman was sweetness through and through.

I stepped out of the car and adjusted my jacket. I wanted to look my best for Rhyannon, so she knew my interest in her was serious.

She'd seemed shocked when I'd asked her out, but I couldn't figure out why. She was gorgeous. And

I was one lucky guy to get the chance to go out with her. I intended to make this the first of many dates if things went well tonight.

I grabbed the bouquet off the passenger seat of my car and headed to the front door. I pressed the bell and waited, sliding my hand down my tie.

The door opened, and my heart stopped. Rhyannon looked gorgeous in a fitted black dress, and she smelled like heaven. How was it fair to my heart that one woman could be so stunning? And that smile. It made me think of an angel.

"Hi, Gabe! You're right on time," she said.

"I'd never keep such a beautiful woman waiting. You look incredible."

"You didn't tell me where we were going, so I didn't want to be dressed in the wrong thing. Is this okay?"

"Every guy in the restaurant will be so jealous that you're on my arm." The longer I kept looking at her, the less I felt able to breathe.

She flapped a hand in the air. "You're making me blush."

I grinned at her. "I got you these. I figured you weren't a traditional flowers kind of woman. Although the florist I ordered them from thought I'd made a mistake."

She stared at the ribbon tied bouquet. "Is that catnip?" She took a sniff of the heart-shaped grayish-green leaves with tiny purple flowers at the end.

"It sure is. I figured the cats needed something to entertain themselves with, while their mom was out having fun."

"Oh! They're perfect. My little ones will love this. Come in. I just need to grab my purse and jacket. And I'd better put this bouquet somewhere safe. If my lot gets unfettered access to it, chaos is guaranteed. And I don't want to come back to the remains of a cat frat party."

I stepped inside and looked around the wide, pale cream entrance hall. There was an old-fashioned feel to it. Everything looked expensive and in good condition, but a little faded around the edges and twenty years out of fashion.

Donut appeared in a doorway. His tail flicked up as if he recognized me. He wobbled his way toward me.

I met him halfway, ducking down to give him a stroke. "How's life treating you, buddy?"

"Meow." His ears lifted, and he looked around.

I followed his gaze. My eyes widened as five cats looked back at me from the doorway. "Hey! Where did you all come from?"

Rhyannon hurried back along the hallway, her purse in one hand. "I'm glad Donut's awake. I didn't like to disturb him. He's been curled up in the laundry basket for hours."

"It looks like the whole gang has come to see us off." I gestured my head at the cats, who watched me with an unsettling intensity. I got the impression I was being judged.

"They're interested in you," Rhyannon said. "We don't get many visitors."

I helped her on with her coat. "They're giving me the stink eye."

She chuckled. "They're curious, that's all. All cats are. It's why they often get in trouble. Grab Donut for me. I need to get his pram."

"He's coming with us?" I looked down at Donut, who blinked up at me with wide, innocent eyes.

"He is. He had trouble walking this morning, and I'm worried about him. I don't want to leave him on his own." She bit her lip. "If you don't want him to come along, we can always rearrange—"

"No! No way. We're going on this date. Bring him along. He's welcome." I'd figure out a way to make sure we snuck Donut into the restaurant.

"Great. I'll be back in a second." She hurried along the corridor again.

I crouched in front of Donut. "Are you really not feeling well, or is this your way of keeping an eye on me to make sure I treat Rhyannon right?" I scooped him up and snuggled him against me.

He nudged my chin with the top of his head and gave a quiet meow.

"You've got nothing to worry about, buddy. I wouldn't do a thing to hurt that sweet woman. She's exactly what I've been looking for. Beautiful, honest, funny, and she sure takes care of you lot, which means she has a heart of gold."

Donut meowed, and several of the other cats echoed him.

I chuckled. "It seems we have an understanding."

Two of the watching cats nodded.

I took a step back. That had to be a coincidence. There was no way they could understand me. "So we're all agreed, I'm here for keeps? Do you all think I'm good enough?"

Donut purred loudly and kneaded the sleeve of my jacket.

I took that to mean he thought me sticking around was a great idea. The others may need a little work.

Rhyannon returned and settled Donut in the pram, then we headed outside.

"I'll go in the back with Donut," Rhyannon said. "He's been in my car plenty of times, but this will be a new experience. We don't usually ride in such luxury."

"Of course." There she was again, being all adorable and thinking about others.

There was plenty of room on the back seat for Rhyannon and the pram, and once they were settled, I drove us to the best restaurant in Silver Birch.

"Here we are." I pulled up in a space right out front.

"Oh! You brought us to Burnaps?" Rhyannon peered at the sign lit in a warm glow.

"I asked around, and people said this was the best place in town. I haven't tried the restaurants here for a while. Will this do?"

"Of course." She glanced at me from beneath those long lashes. "You do know this is a proper date restaurant?"

I laughed. "Well, we are on a proper date, aren't we?"

"Yes, but I figured we'd just go to the diner and chat about the fundraiser."

"We can talk about the fundraiser while we eat here. Are you ready?"

She looked at the restaurant again. "Yep. Sure. Let's do this."

I hopped out of the car, opened her door and helped her out, then extracted the pram.

Donut seemed to be taking in everything with his calm gaze. He didn't mind one bit where we were, so long as he could see Rhyannon.

I caught the eye of the maître d' as we entered the restaurant and nodded at him. "Rhyannon, why don't you go to the bar and order drinks? The table is booked in my name, so just put them on my tab."

"Okay." She went to take the pram.

"I've got this. You get the drinks, and I'll keep an eye on Donut."

She hesitated, her gaze flashing to Donut, then she exhaled. "Is white wine okay?"

"That'll be great." I pushed the pram over to the maître d'. "Hey. I have an emergency situation, and I need your help."

"Of course, sir. How may I assist you?"

"My friend is looking after a sick cat and she can't leave him on his own. This is our first date and I want to make sure things go smoothly. Is there any chance we can bring the cat into the restaurant?"

His nostrils flared, but he ducked down and peered into the pram. "He's a beautiful animal, but I can't allow him in the restaurant."

"Have you got any private rooms? I'm happy to pay, but we need this cat to stay with us. He's important to Rhyannon. She rescued him from Forever Paws. Do you know the place?"

"I do. It's one of my favorite local charities." He studied Donut again. "You know, he looks like my mom's old cat. She was crazy about that raggedy old thing. She called him her third child."

I glanced at the bar where Rhyannon was being served. I was running out of time and there was no way this date would finish before it even got started.

The maître d' scanned the bookings log. "We have a small private meeting room available. It's not currently set for dining, but it won't take more than a couple of minutes to arrange. Would that work for you and your special guest?"

"Yes! That sounds great." I shook his hand. I'd leave a huge tip for this guy. He'd just saved my date.

I wheeled the pram to the bar and took the glass of wine Rhyannon held out for me. "Almost ready. They're just setting up our table."

She looked around, her eyes a little wide. "I... um... I have a confession to make. I've never been here before. I've looked at the menu online plenty of times. The food sounds amazing."

"Surely the guys you dated in the past brought you here."

She bit her bottom lip. "I can't say they have. I haven't been on many dates."

I shook my head. "There must be guys lining up to date you."

Rhyannon looked around. "Hmmm, you need to point that line out to me, because I've been missing it all these years."

How were the guys in Silver Birch not inviting this angel out all the time? "Well, I'm glad they're not bothering you now. It means I get you all to myself."

A pretty flush crossed her cheeks. Rhyannon grabbed two menus off the bar. "Let's look at these whilst we wait." She ducked behind hers, concealing her face from me.

I pretended to study the menu, but the whole time, I was sneaking glances at her. She'd been different in school, quieter, barely saying a word to anyone.

Her friend, Cassie, was more outgoing, which had caught my eye. I wish I'd paid more attention to Rhyannon back then, although I probably wouldn't have treated her right. I'd learned a lot about how to treat a woman since my jock teenage years.

"Do you see anything you like?" I lowered my menu.

"It all sounds good."

I pressed a finger on the top of her menu and lowered it before she had a chance to use it as a shield again. "You look really pretty tonight."

"Thanks. You look nice, too." She reached over and plucked a cat fur off my tie.

"Sir, your table is prepared. If you're ready, I'll show you to your seats." The maître d' gestured for us to follow him.

I grabbed Donut's pram and wheeled it through, entering a small room set just to the right of the entrance. It was perfect. Small, softly lit, and with a romantic vibe.

The gasp from Rhyannon's lips had me turning.

"Is this just for us?"

I nodded as I pulled out her seat. "Only the best for you and Donut."

"Your waitress will be with you in a few moments to take your order." The maître d' nodded at me before leaving the room and closing the door behind him.

We got settled at the table, and Rhyannon looked around. "I never expected this. It's nice. It gives us a chance to talk. I like restaurants, but sometimes get distracted by the chatter and noise going on around me."

"We won't be distracted here. Which is ideal, because I want to know everything about you."

Her gaze lowered. "There's not much to tell. What do you want to know?"

I wanted to know everything. Why Rhyannon wasn't married? What kind of guys she liked? If she saw me as boyfriend material.

I needed to pump the brakes a little, but her kindness had knocked my guard away, and I didn't want to miss my chance with her.

"Let's start with what you do for work," I said. That was a safe, easy topic.

She sighed and smiled, her shoulders dropping. "I work part time at the pet store. Only three days a week. The rest of my time, I volunteer at Forever Paws."

"It sounds like your life is full of animals."

She flipped her napkin onto her lap, a defiant gleam in her eyes as she met my gaze. "I wouldn't have it any other way. Love me, love my cats."

I lifted a hand, charmed by her sass. "You'll hear no complaints from me. The way you care about those animals shows you have a kind heart. I tried to convince Adele we should get a dog, but she was having none of it. She said animals mess up the place and leave fur everywhere."

"Adele is your..."

I winced. I hadn't engaged my brain before opening my mouth. "My ex-girlfriend. My very ex-girlfriend. It was over a while ago."

"It must have been serious if you were talking about getting an animal together." Rhyannon's gaze lowered to the table.

"I thought it was, but things didn't work out. I'm glad of that now I've met you."

A cute smile curled her lips. "I see your high school confidence is still in place."

"You thought I was confident back then?"

"Of course! And you had it so easy. You were in the popular gang, you were a hit on the football team, and all the girls liked you."

I nodded. Those had been the golden days. "And you didn't have it easy?"

"School was okay, but I was glad to move on."

"And I don't remember you getting serious with anyone at school. No high school sweetheart I need to watch out for?"

Rhyannon tweaked the napkin on her lap and chuckled. "Nope. I can't say there is. I was too busy teaching you science and winning in the chess club."

"And now?"

"And now, I'm hopelessly devoted to my cats."

I laughed. "I'm the same when it comes to my relationships, especially the human kind. I'm a one woman guy."

"You don't think there's a chance you'll get back together with Adele if you're such a devoted guy?"

There was that sass again. "That's never happening. Adele never trusted me. Everything was a battle to make her see I could be relied on. It got exhausting."

Rhyannon's eyebrows arched. "Did you give her a reason not to trust you?"

"No. I'm straightforward and honest in a relationship. If I like someone, I tell them. If things go wrong, I work hard to fix them."

"So why didn't she trust you?"

"I wish I could tell you." I shook my head. It was a mystery I'd never solved, and I'd got tired of trying after all the arguing Adele enjoyed so much. "Adele said she wanted the same as me. A simple life, a home, and children."

"That sounds good." That soft wistful lilt to Rhyannon's voice had me smiling.

"I think so." My smile faded. It had been over a year since we'd split, but the memories still sucked. "Then a rich guy turned her head and Adele changed. She stuck the blame on my shoulders to make herself feel better about chasing after a sugar daddy."

Rhyannon wrinkled her nose. "And you're still looking for romance after you got your heart stomped on?"

"It was more like my heart was a little bruised for a while. And being with you makes it feel a hundred times better. In fact, better than new." I patted my chest.

Her lips parted, and she giggled.

It took all my strength not to wrap her in my arms and kiss her. But there'd be time for that once we'd gotten to know each other. I may run into a relationship like a tilting train going at full speed, but I wasn't scaring away Rhyannon.

The door opened, and a waitress entered. "Well, I'll be... Gabe Blackwell! I didn't know you were back in town." She grinned at me.

"Hey! Jessica. Long-time no see," I said.

Jessica Davenport flashed me a megawatt smile, all whitened teeth and glossy lips. "You should have looked me up when you came back. Are you staying long?"

I looked at Rhyannon. She was fidgeting with the menu, her head down. "That's the plan. As long as I'm wanted."

Jessica strode to the table. "We should go out. I can catch you up on everything that's gone on in this place. Although not much has changed."

I remembered Jessica from high school. She'd run fast and loose back then, and it looked like things hadn't changed much. I had no problem with that, it just wasn't my style.

"Thanks for the offer, but I'm going to be busy. Do you remember Rhyannon?"

Jessica finally glanced her way. "Oh, sure."

I reached across the table and took hold of Rhyannon's hand. She flashed me a startled look as her fingers closed around mine.

"We're working on a project together. Raising money for a local charity," I said.

Jessica's eyes hardened as they settled on our joined hands. "Well now, aren't you just a saint?"

"It was Rhyannon's idea. She's the real angel around here. And she's as pretty as one, too."

Jessica pursed her lips. "Whatever you say, honey. Are you two ready to order?"

I looked at Rhyannon, and she nodded.

"It looks like it," I said.

"I'll have the Wheeler's salmon fishcake," Rhyannon said.

"Make that two." I handed Jessica our menus, making sure to keep a tight hold on Rhyannon's hand.

Jessica grabbed the menus. "There'll be a wait. We're busy tonight. The steaks will be quicker."

"I'd prefer the fishcake," Rhyannon said.

I grinned at her. "That's fine. I don't mind a wait. And it means we have more time to get to know each other better."

Jessica huffed out a breath. She turned and left the room, giving the door a good hard slam as she stomped out.

Rhyannon let out a sigh. "I didn't know Jessica worked here."

"Neither did I. You two don't get along?"

"Something like that. In high school, Jessica was..." Rhyannon waved a hand in the air.

"Full of herself? Thought she was better than everyone else? Mean to anyone she felt threatened by?" I said.

She nodded. "Something like that."

"From my memories of Jessica, she only hung out with people if she could get something out of them. She even asked me out a couple of times."

"Did you ever date her?"

"No. Jessica's not my type." I winked at Rhyannon. "My type is sitting right in front of me."

She flashed me a sweet smile. "I figured Jessica was everyone's type."

"Nope. And she doesn't hold a candle to you."

Rhyannon pressed a hand against her cheek. "So, how long are you staying in Silver Birch?"

"This is it, as far as I'm concerned. My work sometimes takes me out of state, but I'll be based here for at least two years while the office renovation happens. We got the contract to do up Brewers."

"Oh! That's great. You do building refits? I'm glad someone is finally investing money into that place. Those buildings used to be beautiful."

"They will be again. We specialize in renovating old properties and bringing them back to life. It'll be a mix of independent stores and affordable apartments."

"I can't wait to see how they look once you're done." She fiddled with her napkin again. "And after that?"

I squeezed her hand. "You want to know if I'm planning on staying in town for good?"

She lifted a shoulder. "I don't mean to pry."

"Of course you do, and I'm glad you asked. It shows you care." And I really wanted this woman to care about me. "I am planning on staying here full time. I love this place. I've got friends here. And now there's the added bonus of you."

Her gaze shot to mine, sending a bolt of something hot into the center of my heart. "You'd stay here for me? But we don't really know each other."

"We used to, and we will again. You're a great reason to stick around."

Her pretty eyes narrowed. "You'd better not be teasing me, Gabe."

"I only tease when the situation is right."

"And is this the right situation?" She lifted her chin, a flicker of adorable defiance in her eyes.

"Rhyannon, we're just getting to know each other again, and I'm loving what I'm learning about you. I feel like a fool for not getting to know you better at school. I feel like I missed out."

She folded her hands in her lap. "You missed out on a heap of fun in chess club. We used to have marshmallow Mondays and sneak in snacks. And there was hot chocolate. We had a riot." Her eyes sparkled with laughter.

"Now I feel like an even bigger idiot for not joining."

"No, you weren't meant for the chess club, just like I wasn't meant for the cheerleading squad. We were feeling our way to adulthood the best way we knew how. We both took a different approach. And if we'd tried being high school sweethearts, it would have gone horribly wrong."

"You think dating me would be horrible?"

"Back then, probably."

"Ouch! And now?"

"I'm still deciding."

I grinned. "My dad always told me when you meet the right girl, something clicks. It happened when he met my mom. They were eighteen and met at a dance in Silver Birch. He looked across the room and there was this vision standing in one corner on her own. I always laugh when he tells me the next bit, but he said she had a glow around her just like an angel. And she was his angel. He went over, asked her to dance, and that was it."

Rhyannon sighed. "That sounds wonderful. Just like the movies."

"They still have their ups and downs, but never go to bed on an argument, and they're always there for each other. That's what I'm looking for." And maybe I'd found it. My heart gave a happy thud.

"I always thought that kind of love could only be found in the movies. I've watched a lot of romance movies and there's always a happily ever after. It doesn't seem so easy in real life."

"The movies glam it all up. Relationships take work. But something that works is worth putting the effort into, don't you think?" I held my hand out to her.

She placed her fingers against mine, and I brushed my thumb across the knuckles, revelling in how soft her skin was.

Those cute dimples in her cheeks popped again, making my heart stutter.

"I never thought about it like that. But you're right. You need to work at something to make it perfect," she said.

"Are you up for a little hard graft with me? I promise you, I'm worth it."

She tipped back her head, and her laugh sent a tingle down my spine. "You're still very sure of yourself, Gabe."

"I am when I'm around you."

Her intense gaze met mine. "So, what kind of place are you looking to buy, or are you going to stick with a rental?"

It felt like a good move to change the topic of conversation. Things were getting intense, and I had to remind myself not to go full steam too soon.

"I'm renting a place from my business partner. He had a one-bed apartment sitting empty and gave it to me at a discount. Having that meant I could settle in straightaway. But I want a house. Is there anywhere you can recommend?"

"There's not much about. Everyone who moves here never wants to leave."

"Yeah, I remember that. Maybe your parents could help me out with new listings that come on their books," I said.

"Oh, no, that won't be possible." She looked away.

I frowned and tilted my head as Rhyannon tensed in her seat. "How about you? Are you saving up for your own place so you can move out of your parents' house?"

Rhyannon withdrew her hand and placed it in her lap again. "No, I live there on my own. That's my home now. I'm not moving."

"But that place is huge for a single person. Where are your parents?"

She bit her bottom lip, and I knew I'd made a big mistake, but it was too late to take it back. "They're not around, anymore. Mom got cancer and Dad, well, I believe he died of a broken heart after he lost her."

"Jeez, I'm such an idiot. I'm so sorry, Rhyannon. I had no idea. You're really in that place all on your own?"

"Of course not. I have my cats. They keep me company."

I grinned. "And there's really no gorgeous guy trying to sweep you off your feet and set up home with you?"

She shook her head. "Nope. I wondered about selling the place after my parents died, but I couldn't face it. There are a lot of happy memories in that house. And they left me well provided for in their will, so I don't need to worry about the upkeep costs or taxes. Although I'd much rather have them alive."

I reached out for her hand again, and she gave it to me. "Of course you would. I'm glad you stayed there. The place suits you."

"It does. And it means I have plenty of room to grow my family."

I almost spluttered out my sip of wine. "You're thinking of having kids?"

"One day," she said on a chuckle. "Right now, I'm thinking about my furry family. Forever Paws is often full, and I offer fostering places to cats who need extra attention."

At that moment, Jessica returned with our food, which she placed in front of us. "Enjoy."

"I, um, mine's cold." Rhyannon pressed a finger on her fishcake.

Jessica's hand was already on the door. She shrugged. "If you want a replacement, it'll be half an hour. We're short-staffed in the kitchen. Oh, and we're all out of fishcakes. Those are the last two. I can always ask Chef to re-heat it, but it'll take a while."

"Send yours back. We can share mine," I said. Jessica was being spiteful by picking on Rhyannon. If she'd treated her like this in school, it was no wonder she hadn't enjoyed her time there.

Rhyannon frowned, but then nodded. "Sure. We can share."

Jessica stalked back to the table and grabbed Rhyannon's plate. She froze as a meow came from the pram tucked by the table. "What in the heck is that?"

I set my hand on top of the pram. "This is Donut."

"Is that a cat?" Jessica's eyes narrowed. "We don't allow animals in the restaurant."

"I cleared it with the maître d'," I said. "He had no problem with Donut coming in with us."

"I do. When the other customers hear about it, they'll complain. It's not hygienic having that thing in here."

"Donut's not a thing, he's a cat. And he's not been well," I said.

"That's not my problem," Jessica said. "I could lose my job if I don't report this."

"You should make it your problem and show a little charity."

Jessica scowled at the pram. "We have health codes to meet. This is a violation."

"We should leave," Rhyannon whispered.

I nodded. "Good plan. Jessica, if you can't be kind about Donut, why don't you come to the fundraiser we're planning at Forever Paws and experience real charity in action?" I gave her a big smile, even though she didn't deserve it. "You could get a cat of your own. Or even make a donation to an amazing cause."

Jessica's nose wrinkled. "I wouldn't waste my time at that place. Those animals should be put down."

Rhyannon sucked in a breath, bright dots of color on her cheeks. "Those animals deserve kindness and fairness. Something you still haven't learned."

I squeezed her hand tightly in a show of support.

"What's that supposed to mean?" Jessica glared at Rhyannon.

She looked over at me. "Let's go."

I nodded as I hopped up and pulled out Rhyannon's chair. "How about the diner?" I whispered in her ear.

"That would be perfect." She gave me a heart-melting smile, before pushing the pram by Jessica without a backward glance.

Jessica stared at me. "What about your food?"

"It looks inedible, and it's cold. We're leaving." I walked out alongside Rhyannon.

The most important thing was to make her happy, and that wasn't happening here. She needed a place that accepted her, cats and all.

And if that meant diner fries and a burger every time we went out on a date, then that's what would happen.

<h1 style="text-align:center">Chapter 9</h1>

Rhyannon

I popped another fry into my mouth and sank back into the padded diner booth seat. I hadn't realized how tense I'd been at that restaurant, especially after I'd set eyes on Jessica Davenport.

Gabe had been amazing. He'd understood I was uncomfortable and had fixed things. Now, we were in my favorite diner, eating cheese loaded fries and drinking rich, delicious chocolate shakes.

I lifted my gaze to Gabe and saw him grinning at me.

"Is everything good?" he asked.

"It is now."

He scooted around the booth until he sat next to me and placed a kiss on my cheek.

I just about melted into my shoes. "What was that for?"

"You're too cute not to kiss."

A heat spread up my neck and onto my cheeks.

"I gotta ask, why aren't you married? You must have turned down a dozen proposals."

I almost choked on my fry. "Hardly. And there are a couple of issues when it comes to getting marriage proposals." I gestured at the pram and then at myself.

His forehead wrinkled. "I don't get it."

"People think if you're a single woman and have cats, there's something wrong with you."

"There is nothing wrong with you," Gabe said. "And the fact you look after unwanted animals is adorable. Why would that put anyone off?"

"It beats me. But guys get this panicked look in their eyes when I tell them I have six cats." I tilted my head. "You didn't do that when you found out about my fur babies."

"Of course not. You volunteer your time to help the vulnerable. You get a big gold star from me. And I'm not going anywhere."

"Which makes you a one-of-a-kind. I can't believe I bumped into you after all this time."

"I'm thrilled it happened."

I dunked a fry into my ketchup. I didn't want to pry, but I had to be sure about something. "And women like Jessica really aren't your taste?" If they were, then I didn't stand a chance with Gabe. We were polar opposites, and I was glad of that.

He gave a low chuckle that had my toes curling. "I admit, back in school, I did a double-take when I saw her in those short skirts she wore. She knew how to please the eye of a teenage boy with out-of-control hormones. But now, not so much. And I seem to remember Jessica got married a few years back."

"Yep, married and divorced," I said. "She cheated on him, so he threw her out of the house."

"Huh! Good for him," Gabe said. "And just to be crystal clear, Jessica is not my taste now. But you, you definitely are."

Oh, my goodness. I needed to get a grip on myself. If I kept staring into those gorgeous eyes and listening to that silky voice say all the right things, I'd never have a straight thought in my head again.

I slid an inch away from Gabe so I wasn't breathing in his woody cologne and getting dizzy. "How about we discuss the fundraiser?"

His grin suggested he knew exactly what I was doing. "Sure. From what you've told me about it, everything is pretty much in place. Although I was thinking I could do something fun. Come dressed up as Santa Claus and bring gifts for the cats. Would they like that?"

"I'm sure they would. Even if they act aloof, cats love presents, especially if it's food or catnip."

"How many cats do I need to play Santa for?"

"There are fifty at the moment. After Christmas, we'll get more, so buying spare gifts would be useful. We're always stretched after the holidays for things like food, blankets, and litter."

"Not a problem. You tell me what they like, and I'll make sure they get it at the fundraiser."

I sat back in my seat. I didn't want to appear pushy, but this was for the cats, so I made myself ask. "As great as gifts are, we need to make sure plenty of people turn up and donate toward the heating system. And I was hoping we might get a few cats adopted, too. This is a great opportunity to showcase the work of Forever Paws and show off our residents who are ready for a new home."

"That makes sense. How many have confirmed they're coming to the event?"

"A hundred so far, but they never all show. I want to double that number. And also make it clear to everyone how desperate Forever Paws is for this new heating. The problem is, I'm no expert at promotion. And I'm much more interested in helping the cats than marketing, even though I know it's important. If people don't know we exist, they won't help. And I have to get them to help. I have to..." I laughed. "I have to stop babbling at you like a genuine crazy cat lady so you don't run for the hills."

Gabe grinned at me. "You can babble all you like. It shows you're passionate, and that's no bad thing. If you need marketing help, I've got just the guy for you. Do you mind if I use my phone while we're at dinner?"

"Of course not." I was touched he bothered to ask. Several of the other couples in the diner seemed more interested in their screens than the partner sitting right in front of them. Gabe had given me his undivided attention all evening, and I was having real trouble not swooning straight into his arms as a result.

"Thanks." He pressed a button on his phone. "Hey, Chris. I need your help."

I tilted my head. Seeing the smile spread across his face as he spoke did strange things to my insides. I hadn't felt this way about a guy in forever. Maybe never. I was so out of practice when it came to relationships.

Gabe winked at me. "This is right up your street. You're our marketing guru, and I know you need Christmas cheer in your life."

Whatever Chris said made him chuckle.

"Remember I told you about my new Christmas mission? Well, it'll need your input." Gabe was quiet for a few seconds as he listened to the other side of the conversation.

I ate another fry and tried not to stare at his upturned mouth.

"All this will cost you is time and good spirit," Gabe said. "It involves cats, Christmas, and your skills in making people drool over what we have to offer."

I leaned closer, eager to hear what Chris thought. There was faint laughter. That was a great sign.

Gabe chuckled in response. "I knew you'd be interested. I'll get Rhyannon to send you the details." He reached over and squeezed my hand. "Yes, I'm with her now, so I'll keep this short. I'll catch up with you tomorrow." He finished the call and placed his phone back in his pocket.

"You have a friend who does marketing?" I asked.

"Yep. Chris Abel. Do you remember him from school?"

"Of course! How did you two get to be friends? Chris used to be in the math club."

"He probably still is in some kind of math club. The guy's a certified genius, but we got talking one evening and realized we had a lot in common."

"You mean to say you like math?"

"Noooo! I hate math, but Chris doesn't like getting his hands dirty and I do, so we're a perfect fit. He deals with the business side of things, and I sweet talk the contractors and make checks on the sites being worked on. Plus, Chris handles all the marketing for my company."

I pressed my hand against my racing heart. This was huge news for the charity. "And he'll help promote the fundraiser?"

"Sure. He's thrilled to do so."

"You're sure we're not putting him out? He must be busy at this time of year. And you have that big contract for Brewer's to focus on."

"We'll be quiet over Christmas. The crews are off now until the new year. They need the break. Working in this cold weather is draining. Besides, Chris is a workaholic. It'll do him good to focus on something else and not Scrooge it up in the office, burning the midnight oil. Besides, how can he complain about doing this? The cats need warm paws all year round."

"This is perfect. And I know Forever Paws will promote your business for helping out." I shifted in my seat. "You could even be a sponsor and make it an official partnership."

Gabe waved his hand in the air. "I'll mention it to Chris, but it's not necessary to promote us. And we do fine without any extra publicity. In fact, we're booked solid for the next couple of years. We couldn't take on extra work even if we wanted to."

"Which means you're going to be busy." My heart sank a little. I'd hope to see a lot more of Gabe now he was back in town.

"I'll never be too busy to spend time with you." His smile made me melt. "Now, how about we finish this food? Then I want to take you somewhere special."

"There's more to this date than fries in my favorite diner?"

"Greasy fries and a milkshake don't make a proper date in my eyes. And I want you to feel special."

I looked around the diner. I already felt special. I was comfortable here, and I could relax and be myself. And as much as I appreciated Gabe's efforts at picking an expensive restaurant, this was much more my style.

He leaned against my arm. "How about you pick the place next time? I'm not much into champagne and caviar either."

"I'd probably want to come back here." I glanced at him. He was suggesting more dates? "Is this place exciting enough for you?"

"Yep. This suits me just fine. They do the best hotdogs in town. And they have the prettiest customers."

I grinned. It felt like I was living in a dream. Getting to know the grown-up version of Gabe was too good to be true. He was everything I wanted in a guy.

Even Donut seemed happy. He was snuggled in the pram and had fallen asleep as soon as we'd arrived. The owner knew me since I was a regular, and was happy for me to bring the cats in, so long as they stayed in the pram.

Gabe paid for our food at the counter, then escorted me out the door, his hand pressed against the small of my back, sending shivers of delight up my spine.

He held the car door open for me, settled Donut gently next to me, then slid into the driver's seat.

"Where are we going?" I asked.

"You'll know soon enough. It's not far." He started the engine and pulled out of the parking space, before heading up the hill toward the center of Silver Birch.

His gaze met mine in the rearview mirror and he smiled.

Every time that happened, my insides got warm, and I started imagining all the possibilities we could have together. It was a silly dream, but Gabe seemed like a straightforward, honest guy. If he liked something, he said he did, and made it clear when he didn't approve of bad behavior.

He was a straight up and down solid guy. Exactly what I'd been looking for all my life. Could I have found my perfect match with a former high school jock I tutored in science?

"This is us." He pulled into the parking lot of the high school and killed the engine.

I pulled a face as I looked around the empty lot. "What are we doing back at school?"

"It's the highest spot in town. And it's a full moon tonight. I thought it would be nice to sit and watch."

I pursed my lips. "You do know this is a make out spot? The kids think it's daring to sneak onto school property and lock lips."

Gabe shot me a wicked grin that had me heating up all the way to my hairline. "The thought had crossed my mind." He undid his seatbelt and came around to my door, opening it for me.

I grabbed his outstretched hand and stepped outside. I took a moment to stare at the clear dark night sky, glad of the cool air to chill my hot cheeks. "There's no sign of snow tonight."

"We've had enough of that. We'll still have a white Christmas, though." His arm slipped around my waist and he held me close. "I spent a lot of happy days in this place."

I leaned against him. "I had a few happy days, but I was glad to leave. High school's not the easiest place when you aren't in the popular crowd."

His grip tightened on my waist. "High school cliques are the worst. I wish I'd been a part of the chess club and spent all my time with you."

I thumped him gently on the chest, hitting a wall of solid muscle. "You do not. You were a jock, and I was a chess geek. We found our tribe and stuck with it. High school isn't the place to go exploring and take risks by swapping groups. Otherwise, you end up an outcast. We were both doing what we needed to do to survive."

"I reckon you survived just fine. You've grown into a beautiful, sweet woman who's got the world at her feet."

"I'm not so sure about that," I said softly.

Being out here with Gabe, just the two of us, it did feel like a whole world of possibilities was before me. His firm grip around my waist and the feel of his warmth seeping into me filled me with contentment.

Neither of us spoke for some time, simply looked up into the night sky.

It wasn't until I shivered that Gabe moved away from me. "Let's get back in the car."

This time, I sat in the passenger seat next to him, and we watched the huge full moon rise slowly in the sky, while the heater in the car kept us toasty warm.

"Somehow, this doesn't seem real. It's like a fairy tale." I tensed. That thought had spilled out before I'd monitored it.

Gabe shifted in his seat. "This is real to me. And I like you, Rhyannon. I liked you when you taught me all the chemical symbols on the periodic table, and I like you even more now. You were a kind person back then. I was the idiot who missed out on that kindness."

"You missed nothing."

"I missed you."

I kept my gaze on the moon. This didn't feel like a setup. Gabe's tone was sincere, as were his eyes, but I needed to know I wasn't just something to pass the time. I didn't do casual relationships. "When you met Adele, was it love at first sight?"

Gabe was silent for several seconds. "I'm not sure. No, I don't think it was. Do you believe in that?"

"I'm not sure, either. My parents had a great marriage, but the way they met was horribly practical. Did I ever tell you the story?"

"No, you never talked much about your parents."

"Well, hold on to your hat. This is straight out of Practical Husband Seeking monthly magazine."

"That's a thing?"

I laughed. "No! But my mom put an announcement in the paper outlining the kind of guy she wanted to marry. She was very clear. No time wasters allowed."

He turned in his seat, the disbelief on his face making me chuckle. "She advertised for a husband? What offers did your mom get?"

"Plenty of strange ones, all of which she turned down. But she had a list of things she expected from her husband. She'd take it with her on each date and go through every line. If the guy she was on the date with didn't match up to those standards, then that was the end. He didn't get a second chance."

"Whoa! Your mom was a little terrifying."

"She was at times, but also amazing. I admired her. She knew exactly what she wanted and went after it until she got it. And Mom found her perfect guy."

"How long did it take her to find your dad?"

"Eighteen months. She kept the same ad in the paper and would simply add at the bottom: *former applicants need not reapply*."

Gabe roared with laughter. "That's awesome. And your dad finally answered the ad?"

"He did. He said it was the toughest interview of his life. Mom sat there with the list in front of her, calmly sipping a coffee and telling him everything she expected from her man."

"Was he fine about that? Did he have his own list of demands?"

"Dad always wanted a woman who knew her own mind and didn't stand for any nonsense. He loved her. He loved her spirit, her calm ways, and her determined focus."

"And the way she terrified him?"

I giggled. "She maybe scared him a bit. Mom said that after she'd interviewed him for two hours and they'd gone on a dozen dates, she was satisfied she could develop affection for him."

"Affection? It sounds more like a practical arrangement than true love."

"Peoples views on love differ." I glanced at him. "Some people want the whoosh-bang of instant chemistry, and some want the slow burn that never dies."

"Can't you have both?"

"Maybe. Although I've never found both in a relationship." Sitting here with Gabe so close, with my heart racing, made me wonder exactly what I'd found with him. This felt much more than friends. This was exciting. Could it endure? Could it even get started?

"But you'd like to?" he asked.

"Um... sure. Everyone wants to be loved, and to find true love."

Gabe nodded. "I do. I don't suppose you've got a scary list like your mom had that you want to run past me? I'm happy to interview for the position. If it's open."

I swallowed, careful to keep my expression composed. "Maybe it is. I'll see if you pass the first round of questions."

"I'll study hard to make sure I do."

I grinned at him. Gabe was already down to the final round. And he was the only candidate I'd been interested in for a long time. "I'm not as practical as my mom. And sometimes, I wished she was a bit more open with her feelings. I think that's why I love watching romance movies so much. Mom and Dad cared for each other and they were a great fit, but it was never the magic I see in the movies."

"There can be plenty of magic if you want it." He reached over and took my hand. "And while we've been talking, I've been thinking. I do believe it's possible to see someone for the first time and for something magical to happen. I also think people reckon they fall in love at first sight, but there's something more primal going on."

"You mean lust?"

"I definitely do. And that's no bad thing if you're not looking for someone to spend your life with."

My heart ricocheted so loudly in my chest, I was certain he'd hear. "And what are you looking for?"

"I've been looking for that special someone for a while. I was cautious after my last relationship failed. I figured I'd messed up. But I hadn't. It just wasn't meant to be. And I'd have needed a much bigger bank balance to keep Adele happy."

I shook my head. "I don't care if you're rich or poor."

Gabe's smile softened. "Yeah, I figured you wouldn't. And I'm not letting my past setbacks stop me from finding the right one."

"That's good to know." I did that. I held back and kept out of the limelight. Being the center of attention was scary, but if you hid from life, no-one would ever notice you.

"How about you?"

"Huh? What do you mean?"

"I mean, have you ever met a guy who's left you breathless? Made you imagine a long and happy future with him?"

There was a question and a half. I'd been having all sorts of crazy thoughts like that since meeting Gabe again. Some verged on ridiculous fantasies, but the more time I spent with him, the more grounded they seemed. I could see a future with him.

"There's been no one special in my life. No one I thought I could spend the rest of my life with," I said carefully.

"Is that so?" There was a gentle, teasing tone to his voice. "I'd love to change that. So long as I pass the interview."

"Hmmm. I need to give that some serious thought."

He chuckled. "You're more like your mom than you realize. You may not have an actual physical list, but you know what you want and you're not accepting anything less. And you're not wasting your time dating guys who are placeholders for the real thing."

I nodded as I turned over his words. As practical as I tried to be about relationships, I desperately wanted the fireworks, the magic, and everything that came with the glow of true love. Could this be the start of what I'd always been looking for?

I stared at the huge moon that lit the night sky. "Thanks for bringing me here. It's stunning. I've had a great time this evening."

"Having you by my side beats it all. I've had the best time tonight with you, even with the terrible waitress service and the dodgy fishcake."

I looked at him and smiled, my breath coming out a little shaky. "Same here. But we should get going. It's getting late and everyone back home will be wondering where I am."

"Of course. We can't forget the fur babies."

"I'll never forget them," I said. "And they'll expect extra attention and food because they were left on their own all evening."

He tilted his head. "You spend most of your evening with the cats?"

I looked away. Was I about to be judged for my lack of social life? I pulled back my shoulders. It was my life, and I was good with that. "That's right. Will that be an issue?"

"Noooo! And relax, I was just checking. I'm always content with a night on the couch with a movie."

"And a load of cats jostling to get the best spot on that couch?"

"Always. Them, too. So long as you're there." He nudged me with his shoulder. "And if you ever want to spend a whole day with me, we can always hire someone to sit with the cats. I don't want you to worry about them."

I nodded. I knew several friends from Forever Paws who'd love that job. "That's a great idea. That could work."

"Perhaps you can treat them to some of the catnip when you get back, to make up for being out."

I grimaced. "If I do that, none of them will sleep. I'll have a house full of hyperactive cats all night racing around and chasing each other. They can get a treat in the morning."

"You're the boss, my beautiful, crazy cat princess." Gabe kissed the back of my hand and then started the engine.

I'd take the crazy cat princess label, especially since he'd called me beautiful.

The drive back to my house was short, but I could already feel tiredness settling over me. It had been a long time since I'd been on such a fun date. Maybe I'd never enjoyed myself so much with a guy.

Gabe climbed out and lifted the pram out the back, before pushing it to the front door for me.

I turned to face him. "I had a great time tonight. Thanks for taking me out."

His hand on my waist had my heart stuttering. "It was the best date I've ever been on."

I grinned up at him. "You really can't beat the fries at the diner."

"I meant being with you." He leaned down toward me.

I swallowed and licked my lips. I never expected a kiss from Gabe, but I wanted one.

His gaze met mine, and he stilled. "You really are pretty. I'm such a fool for not noticing until now."

"We were both a little foolish when growing up. I was too shy, and you..."

"Was a jock who thought he knew it all. How wrong could I be?" His lips pressed lightly to mine.

For a second, I couldn't see straight. I held him close, my heart pounding.

Gabe stepped closer, pressing me against his chest, and the kiss deepened.

"I've been thinking about kissing you all night." His words were just a whisper against my lips, before he kissed me again.

Holy smokes. No man had ever kissed me like that before. It wasn't the first time I'd been kissed, but Gabe knew what he was doing. It was the perfect amount of passion and pressure, and his grip was secure, making me feel safe.

When we finally broke apart, my knees were shaking. "That was..." my words failed me.

"Worth the wait." He pressed a kiss to my forehead.

"Absolutely." Should I invite him in? I wanted more kisses, but this was a first date. "Um... what now?"

His grin was wolfish. "As much as I don't want to be a gentleman and stand out here kissing you until the sun comes up, we've both got busy days tomorrow."

I sighed and leaned against his chest. He was such a temptation. What was I getting myself into?

"I can't resist you for much longer if I stay here. But before I go..."

I squeaked as he lifted me off my feet and pressed more kisses to my lips.

Gabe kissed me like he couldn't get enough of me, and I was more than happy to reciprocate.

When he finally set me back on my feet, I was dizzy and smiling, and trying really hard not to giggle.

"Well," he whispered, "you, Miss Sitterly, are just what I've been waiting for."

I nodded and grinned. I couldn't be falling for Gabe so quickly. I mean, I knew him, but not like this. And now, he'd just about clubbed me over the head with a love stick, and I was a goner.

I repressed a groan. Too many romantic movies had addled my brain.

I was in trouble. And if I wasn't careful with my heart, it would be lost to Gabe forever.

Chapter 10

Gabe

Do you like eggnog? I grinned as I sent the message to Rhyannon.

The response was instant. *Yuck. Drinking egg. NO. How about mulled wine?*

I laughed while I typed a reply. It had been five days since I'd seen Rhyannon on our date, and I kept finding excuses to text or call her every day. It was hard to stay away from her. And why should I? She was an amazing woman, she was single, and she'd gotten my heart all twisted up.

Every time we talked, she just seemed to get sweeter and funnier.

She'd been in my thoughts all the time, and I needed to find a way to make sure she stayed in my life permanently.

I'd fallen hard for this Christmas angel who loved cats more than people, and I wanted the world to know about it.

Snowy Christmas or sunny Christmas? Rhyannon texted.

Whatever you like. So long as you're by my side, I won't notice the snow or the sun. I'll already have the best view just by looking at you.

Cheese ball.

It's your fault. You make me like this. Affection pulled through me as she sent back several kisses.

If I needed another reason to come back home for good, I'd just found it in Rhyannon. I was ready to make someone my forever. I wanted someone who trusted me and who I could trust right back. I still struggled to see the best in people after the number Adele had pulled on me, but with Rhyannon, she made it easy.

She'd been honest with me from the get go. She'd shown me what she loved and what her passions were and hadn't hidden them. She knew her path in life, and I admired that.

A tap on the window of my car had me looking up. Chris stood outside, the collar of his coat pulled up against the brisk winter wind.

Speak soon. I sent the quick message to Rhyannon, before hopping out of the car.

Chris narrowed his gaze. "What are we doing meeting here?" He gestured a thumb over his shoulder at the luxury car lot.

"You know how much fun you had when I took you to see all those cars a couple of months ago?"

"You mean, the three long, exhausting weekends of me watching you test drive almost identical cars, before choosing the first one you tried out?"

I laughed. "I'm glad you have such fond memories of our time together."

"As if I could forget." He glanced at the car. "Is there a problem with it? There can't be. It's almost new."

I patted the hood. I did love this car, but it no longer felt important. Not now I had a bigger mission to focus on.

"Uh-oh. I don't like that look in your eyes. What are you about to do?" Chris's gaze went back to the car lot.

"I'm selling my wheels back to the dealership," I said.

He staggered back, his hand going to his chest. "You've only just got this baby. Is there really something wrong with her?"

"She's great. Better than great. But…"

Chris groaned. "It's a woman. It's got to be. Please don't tell me Rhyannon's insisted you get a people carrier for all the disgustingly cute babies you're going to produce?"

I chuckled. I may have mentioned Rhyannon to him once or twice since our date. And the thought of having children with Rhyannon lit up my insides. She'd be the perfect mom.

"Rhyannon's not said a thing about the car," I said. "Selling the car wasn't her idea."

"I don't get it." Chris shoved a hand through his hair. "You don't like how she handles?"

"The car handles like a dream. But my new Christmas mission needs the money."

"Whoa! Wait a second. I know what this is all about. You're selling the car to help the animal shelter. The shelter Rhyannon is obsessed with."

I grinned. "You got it. It'll mean so much to Rhyannon that they get the heating in place this winter."

"Do you really have to do this? What about all the freebies you've mooched off me this past week to promote the fundraising event? Won't that get Rhyannon the money she needs?"

"Nope. She's done an amazing job with the fundraiser, and it'll definitely raise some of the money, but it won't be enough. And supplying heating for a massive place like that is expensive. She showed me the costings the other day."

Chris shook his head. "You're selling your dream car to keep cats warm. I can't decide if that's lame or awesome?"

"I'm picking awesome. And Rhyannon will love it. So will I. I can get a run around, or use a work's van if I need wheels in the short term. It doesn't matter to me."

Chris grinned. "Rhyannon's got your heart flipped around the wrong way. I've never seen you like this before. You seem all turned around."

I returned his grin and slapped his shoulder. "It feels like it's all turned around the right way for the first time."

"So this is what you look like when you're head-over-heels for a woman. And may I say you've made an awesome choice with the woman of your dreams."

"Yeah and don't I know it. Rhyannon's amazing." I nudged him toward the office on the luxury car lot. "Come on, let's do the painful paperwork and sell this car back before I change my mind."

Half an hour later, I walked away from the car lot minus a car and a whole heap of money being deposited into my account. It felt great. It was another step closer to giving Rhyannon her Christmas wish.

Chris headed to his own car. "I guess this means you need a ride."

"That's the only reason I asked you here."

He shook his head. "You're such a douchebag. Where to?"

"Well, I had an idea while we were making the deal. I got more from the dealership than I thought I would." I slid into the seat next to him.

"You got a great deal because you've barely used it. I bet he'll put a ten percent mark up on that baby and have her sold by the end of the day." Chris glanced at the office. "If you're quick, you could go in and snatch the paperwork back. Say you've changed your mind."

"Nope. I've got a much better plan. Let's hit the pet store. The huge one on the retail park on the east side of town."

Chris's jaw dropped. "Did you mistake the word bar for pet store?"

I chuckled. "No, you heard me right. And we can chill later. I want to get the cats something special for Christmas."

"Crazy cat guy alert," Chris muttered under his breath. "You do know you have fur on your tie?"

"It adds to the look. And quit it with the jibes. Those cats don't get much being in the shelter, and they'll appreciate an extra gift. You can even help me pick out the squeaky mice and snuggle blankets."

"Snuggle blankets? Are you the same Gabe Blackwell I used to know?"

"No, I'm the new and improved version. And Rhyannon's cats are cool. What the shelter does is amazing."

"Yeah, I'm not arguing that point. I've spoken to a woman called Mulberry there several times while we finalize the fundraising publicity. She's as crazy about rescue cats as you. She keeps sending me pictures via email of all the cats up for adoption."

"That's a great idea. You have to get a cat."

"No way. I'm a busy working guy. Besides, it's not manly to get a kitty."

"It's not manly to ignore their plight."

Chris groaned. "You're impossible."

I laughed. "And I expect you to make a huge donation at the event."

"Anything else? You've already got free promotion for the charity event, now you want a donation to the cats, and for me to be your personal chauffeur. Am I your buddy, or your servant?"

"You can be both. You're great at filling those roles." Chris was a true friend. He didn't mind helping out, even though he protested. He was only in his Christmas Scrooge mode.

He grunted as we drove away from the car lot. "I would never have put you and Rhyannon together, but she seems important to you."

My heart swelled as an image of Rhyannon filled my thoughts. "She's possibly the most important person I've ever met."

"More important than Adele?" Chris slid a glance my way. "You two got serious for a while. I figured you were heading for marriage."

I dropped my head back against the seat. "This feels a hundred times more important. This is so different from what I had with Adele. When we were together, she made me doubt myself. Made me think I wasn't good enough for her. I offered her everything she asked for, and she still demanded more. When I couldn't give it to her, she found a guy who could."

"If it's any consolation, I hear she's real unhappy with her new squeeze. Apparently, he works all hours and leaves her on her own all the time."

"I'm sorry if that's the case. Adele messed me around, but no one should get their heart squashed."

"You're way too good of a guy for Adele."

"Heck, yeah! I'm a good guy. I'm an awesome guy."

"And you just ruined it by being a douche again," Chris said.

I chuckled. "I know one thing is true out of all this. Good guys definitely don't finish last."

"From that smile on your face, it looks like you've won the race already," Chris said. "Is it official between you two yet?"

"It is as far as I'm concerned. I know it's only been a week since we reconnected, but there's something big here. We share a past, and there are so many connections that link us. When she smiles at me, man, something happens."

Chris grimaced. "You've been watching too many chick flicks."

"You should try them. Rhyannon's got a huge collection. We're planning a movie marathon soon. Maybe we could double-date."

"I'll think about that. Although seeing that dopey grin on your face almost makes the threat of a chick flick marathon worth exploring if I can snag some of that happiness."

"You'll find your perfect woman. And I'm all in as far as Rhyannon's concerned." My heart gave a happy thud about that fact.

The traffic slowed, and we joined a long queue to get into the retail park. "You know the world and his tinsel covered wife will be shopping here for Christmas gifts?" Chris said.

"Stop complaining and suck up some Christmas spirit. We're doing this for the unloved cats of this world." I flicked on some Christmas tunes. "Let's go make some cats happy."

Chapter 11

♥

Rhyannon

"All the food is out, the guests will start arriving in half an hour, and the donation buckets are waiting to be filled." I looked around the reception area of Forever Paws, my insides jangling like Christmas bells with anticipation.

Mulberry wrapped an arm around my shoulders. She wore another one of her amazing cat themed sweaters. "You haven't stopped for five minutes. Here, have this." She handed me a mug of hot chocolate.

"Thanks. This is just what I need." I took a sip of the sugary warmth. "Do you think we're ready? Have I missed anything?"

"No, it all looks perfect. It's incredible how much you've done in such a short space of time. You're the animals' miracle worker. And we've got over five hundred people planning to visit. I hope we can fit everyone in."

"So do I. And I had a little help to get everything done." I glanced over my shoulder and a thrill of happiness spun through me as Gabe wrestled with an enormous sack of gifts he'd brought in.

He'd even enlisted his best friend and business partner, Chris, to help, and they were busy debating which presents to give the cats.

My heart gave a flutter as I considered how he'd bent over backward to make this a perfect event. I couldn't have wished for anything more. He'd proven time and again that I could rely on him, and he was devoted to making this work. And maybe he was also devoted to me.

Gabe glanced up, caught my eye, and the smile he gave me made everything fade. All I could see was him.

Mulberry squeezed my shoulder, an amused gleam in her eyes. "Rhyannon? What do you think?"

I looked away from Gabe and blushed. I'd missed everything Mulberry had just said. "Sorry, I was miles away."

"Maybe you weren't that far away." Mulberry grinned warmly. "That young man of yours is helpful to have around."

"He's been great. He's worked so hard in getting gifts for all the cats."

"It'll be a wonderful surprise for them," Mulberry said. "Gabe is making this magical Christmas time even more special for everyone."

"You're right. It really feels like there's magic in the air." I'd been on my own for a long time and maybe retreated from the world after my parents died. I'd sought solace in the things I loved, and they'd helped heal my heart, but I hadn't realized there was still a part that needed mending. Not until

Gabe had re-entered my life and shown me how wonderful it felt to be wanted.

"Meow?" Donut wobbled over to me.

"Come here, sweetie." I'd been keeping him with me as much as possible, and he always loved his outings to Forever Paws in the cat pram.

I knelt as he approached, running a critical gaze over his movements. "What do you think, Mulberry? Is Donut getting better?"

"I see definite signs of improvement. He hasn't turned in a circle since he's been here."

A tendril of hope fastened around my heart. Donut was recovering. Slowly but surely his health was improving, as was his confidence around people. I felt optimistic he'd make a complete recovery. It would be a wonderful Christmas gift if he did.

I scooped Donut into my arms and snuggled him against me. I was rewarded with a heart melting purr as he looked up and blinked at me. "I think you'll enjoy the fundraiser, but remember you can always sneak into your pram if you need a little downtime."

Donut meowed again, before he looked straight at Gabe.

"What do you think of Gabe?" I whispered.

"Meow." It was the loudest noise he'd ever made as he blinked at me several times.

"I think that's an approving sounding meow," I said.

"Of course it is." Mulberry stroked Donut's head. "Cats know when goodness runs through a person. Gabe's energy is a hundred percent positive. And it'll soon be time to find him a cat of his own."

"Do you think he's ready to adopt? It would be great if he could offer one a home."

"Oh, I'm certain there'll be more than one cat in Gabe's life in the very near future," Mulberry said. "The cats keep whispering to me that he's got a heart big enough to give a lot of love."

My toes curled at the thought of receiving Gabe's love. I hadn't known what I was missing until he walked back into my life and opened his heart to me. Gabe had also given my heart a gentle shove, reminding me how exhilarating romance could be.

He hadn't hidden his interest. He'd pursued me, but hadn't been pushy, giving me time to get to know him all over again.

"I must go and check on the new arrivals in Cat Alley." Mulberry nodded at me. "We don't want them getting stressed because of our big event." She gave Donut one more tickle before heading off.

After a final snuggle with Donut, I carefully placed him down. He sat and seemed content to wash his face as the final touches to the event happened around him.

I'd just grabbed a large box of donations and was taking them to the storeroom, when the main door to Forever Paws opened.

My heart froze along with my feet as Jessica waltzed through the door. Her gaze flicked around, and her expression suggested she wasn't pleased with what she saw. Then she spotted Gabe, and a huge smile crossed her face. She stalked over to him in her sky high heels. How had she walked through the snow in shoes that impractical? And what was she doing tottering over to Gabe?

I swallowed, my heart thundering as I placed the box back down. When Gabe told her about the fundraiser, she'd practically sneered in his face.

My stomach flipped, an unsettling sickness filling me as she stopped right beside Gabe and threaded her hand through his elbow.

He turned, surprise clear in his eyes as he looked down at her, a cautious smile crossing his face.

I wasn't close enough to hear what she said, but from the flip of her hair and the light laughter that drifted toward me, it was clear she was flirting.

A hot ball of pain lit in my gut. Jessica knew I was dating Gabe. And although her gaze passed right over me as she'd looked around, she'd seen me. She knew I was here, yet didn't care I could see her flirting with my guy.

My guy! Yes, Gabe was mine. We'd not talked about our relationship status, but I wasn't interested in anyone else.

A pained noise shot out of me as Jessica flung her arms around Gabe's neck and planted a kiss on his lips. The world felt like it tilted beneath my feet, and I grabbed the counter beside me and tried to suck air into my lungs.

Donut lowered his ears and hissed in Jessica's direction.

Gabe had already stepped away from Jessica and was shaking his head.

I swallowed the lump in my throat. But I wasn't sad. I was raging mad. How dare she make a move on my guy!

Gabe's gaze shot to mine, and horror filled his face. He strode over to me.

I lifted a hand as he got close. "Just give me a minute."

"Rhyannon! I have no idea why Jessica kissed me, and I don't want to know. I'm not interested in her. I didn't encourage her."

I kept my hand up, rage and anger pulsing through me. And there was also a strong desire to walk over to Jessica and bop her right on the nose.

Gabe touched my arm. "Trust me. I'd never hurt you. That wasn't what it looked like."

"Yes, it was! I saw what happened." The image of Jessica's brazenness was seared into my brain.

His face paled. "No! I'd never betray you. I... Rhyannon, I love you."

Those three little words almost knocked me off my feet. I stared up at him. We'd only been dating a few weeks. Was it too soon to talk about love? "You... love me?"

He grabbed my hand and squeezed tight. "This may sound crazy, but my dad always said I'd know when I met the right woman. And I have. It's you. I knew almost the second we met on that freezing street corner and you stopped to talk to those homeless guys. You're special. You're one-of-a-kind."

"Wait! Dial this conversation back a few lines. You just said you love me. Did you mean it?"

A smile slid across his face, joining the caution in his eyes. "I did. And I do. You're what I've been looking for. You've been here this whole time, and I was too much of an idiot to realize what was waiting for me, right here, back in my hometown. I love this place, and I love you."

"I... I mean, wow!" My mind was too scrambled to form a sentence.

"Don't be angry with me. Jessica made a mistake. It won't happen again. I made that clear."

"Stop! Just let me get everything in the right order." I took a step back and looked at Gabe. I really looked. I had to see all of him. His kindness, his faithfulness, his devotion and passion for helping me and the cats I cared about so deeply.

"Are you angry with me?" Wariness entered his eyes.

My heart caught and swelled. "No, I'm not angry with you. Gabe, I trust you. I just needed a minute to calm down. Otherwise, Jessica would be on her back after I'd slugged her, and I don't want to get arrested just before Christmas."

"Oh! Ohhhhh!" A startled laugh shot out of him. "You're mad at her?"

"Of course! I saw everything. Jessica had no right to do that. She came here to cause trouble. You did nothing wrong." I took his hand. "And, just so you know, I love you, too."

"You do?" Gabe's grin grew goofy, and he lowered his mouth to mine.

I knew where he was heading, but needed to deal with something before I lost myself in his kisses. "Hold on to that thought." I pressed a finger against his lips.

He groaned. "Do I have to?"

"This isn't exactly a private place." I glanced around and blushed. Mulberry was standing behind the reception desk, sneaking glances as she pretended to study a piece of paper in front of her. Chris was on the opposite side of the room, grinning broadly and not doing anything to disguise the fact he was watching. Jessica stood next to him, shooting daggers at us.

Gabe cleared his throat. "I get your point. Shall we go—"

"You stay right here. There's something I have to do."

"Nope. I go where you go." Gabe clamped an arm around my waist. "We're in this together."

"Then let's go speak to Jessica." The all-encompassing love I felt for Gabe had replaced my anger. Jessica could do nothing to hurt us. She could try to make me doubt myself and my relationship, but she'd fail.

I walked over to her, confident with Gabe's arm tucked around my waist.

Her glare went from me to Gabe. "You're kidding? This is a real thing? I figured you'd taken Rhyannon out on a sympathy date."

I'd need to reconsider the whacking her option if she kept talking like that. I was no-one's sympathy date.

"I'm not kidding about Rhyannon," Gabe said. "She's my girl."

Jessica smirked and tossed her long hair over one shoulder. "You're picking cat lady over me?"

"Always and forever."

My head shot around and I stared up at him, forgetting all about Jessica for a second. "Forever? That's a long time."

"Yup, if you'll have me." Gabe had never sounded more sure of anything since I'd met him.

"Of course, I'll have you. I mean, are you sure?"

"I always have been about you. Ever since that first snowy night when we reconnected." He grinned down at me.

As much as I wanted to lose myself in his gaze, I pulled my attention back to Jessica who was still sneering at me.

It was time she learned a lesson in the girl code book. "You touch my guy again and there'll be trouble."

"Trouble from you?" She crossed her arms over her chest, not looking impressed.

"Yes. I'm with Gabe. We're together and happy, and no one's taking that away from us."

"How are you going to stop me?" Jessica tossed a seductive smile at Gabe. "Guys are all the same. And I know what they really want."

Gabe opened his mouth as if to protest, but I patted his arm. I wasn't scared of Jessica anymore.

"Rhyannon will have help, although I'm sure she won't need it." Mulberry appeared by my side. "Gabe is an honest man, he won't let her down. And he won't be tempted by you. Rhyannon is popular in Silver Birch. She's kind and looks out for others. Therefore, there will be lots of people keeping an eye on you, to make sure you don't cause any trouble in their relationship."

"Awww! You've got Mrs. Claus on your side. A middle-aged bore and a dull cat crazy spinster are hardly a threat." Jessica yelped and jumped sideways.

Donut stood behind her, calmly licking his paw.

"It attacked me!" Jessica grabbed the back of her ankle. "That thing needs to be destroyed. It's not safe around people."

"Did you see Donut attack?" Mulberry turned to me, a picture of wide-eyed innocence.

I shook my head. "He never bites or scratches. He's a big softie."

"The blood on my leg says otherwise." Jessica scowled at me. "Gabe, do something. These people are crazy. And you can't want to spend the rest of your life with her."

"I do. It's time you left, Jessica," Gabe said. "I get the impression this is the wrong place for you. Maybe you're more a dog person."

Jessica glared at me, then threw her hands up in the air. "Fine. I wasn't that interested in Gabe, anyway." She turned and stomped away.

"Babe, even I got a little scared at the death glare you just shot at Jessica," Gabe said. "Remind me never to make you angry."

"You can make me angry, just so long as you make up for it afterward." I pressed a kiss to his cheek, then turned to Mulberry. "Thanks for the backup."

"It was my pleasure. Nothing gets in the way of true love when I have anything to do with it." She smiled at me and Gabe.

I scooped up Donut and gave him a big snuggle. "You're such a good boy."

He purred and nuzzled my chin with the top of his head.

"This little furry family is too adorable to be true," Chris said.

I smiled at Gabe, my heart happy and full to the brim with love. "Yes, we really are."

I had my guy, my cat, and my friends around me. Life couldn't get any better.

<h1 style="text-align:center">Chapter 12</h1>

<h1 style="text-align:center">Gabe</h1>

The warm, happy glow that filled my heart when Rhyannon had told me she loved me was still there, shining brightly. I tucked her hand in mine and squeezed, thrilled when she shot me a sweet smile.

How had I gotten so lucky? If that had been Adele witnessing Jessica plant a smacker on me, she'd have laid into me and blamed me for leading Jessica on. But Rhyannon had seen straight through Jessica's games. She'd seen the truth. And she trusted me.

And I trusted her right back. Rhyannon had my heart. She had my everything.

"How you doing up there, buddy?" I moved Donut's front paws around my neck so he was a little closer as he slid back.

He'd been curled around me for the last couple of hours, ever since the confrontation between Rhyannon and Jessica. He'd played his part beautifully and was an awesome little fighter, helping to send Jessica away with her tail between her legs.

He seemed to enjoy being up high so he could watch the buzzing crowd come through the doors at Forever Paws as they took part in the Christmas fun, spun the tombola, hooked a bottle, bought homemade gifts, and made their donations.

"I can't believe how well this is going." Rhyannon's smile nearly took my breath away. "And there are still more people coming into the parking lot. It's almost full out there."

"I'll take my thank you in a large glass of mulled wine and one of those mince pies before they all go." Chris strolled over, looking smug.

"You don't need thanking. You're doing this because you're a charitable guy who likes to help those less fortunate," I said.

He lifted a shoulder. "Maybe that's true. But I wouldn't mind a mulled wine and something sweet, either."

"Of course. Let me get that for you," Rhyannon said. "It's my small way of thanking you for everything you've done to help."

I tugged her back to my side before she'd even taken a step. "Chris can get his own mulled wine."

Chris rolled his eyes. "Is there anything you won't do for Rhyannon? You give up your free time to help out with this event, you spend your money on getting gifts for the cats, you sell your car—"

I coughed loudly and shook my head at him. But the secret was out.

"Wait! What was that about your car?" Rhyannon turned to me, shock in her eyes. "You sold it?"

I glared at Chris, who lifted a hand in apology, before I turned to Rhyannon. "I decided the car wasn't for me."

"But you were so proud of that car. You showed it off to me the night we met. I don't understand."

"Gabe wanted to make sure you reached your fundraising target for Forever Paws," Chris said, seeming oblivious to my continued death stares. "He took the car to the dealer and sold it back to him."

Rhyannon gasped. "You didn't have to do that. Tonight will raise a good few thousand more toward the new heating system."

"It's fine. I wanted to do it. And I felt bad sitting in my flash heated car seat while the cats were here getting cold. It only seemed right."

A choked laugh shot out of Rhyannon. She flung her arms around my neck and kissed me in front of everyone.

I kissed her right back, grinning once we pulled apart. "I did a good thing?"

"You did an incredible thing. Are you for real? With this extra money, we'll meet the target straightaway."

"I am for real. And I'm all yours. I was planning to surprise you with the news at the end of the event. But..." I gestured my head at Mr. Motor Mouth.

Chris grinned. "The cats will get their Christmas heating after all."

Mulberry bustled over, her cheeks gleaming and fluffy Christmas baubles hanging off each ear. "Chris! You're just the man I want to see."

Chris stared at her. "Me?"

"I've been watching you. Something is missing in your life, which I can help to fulfil."

He shot a panicked look my way. "Um, I'm really flattered, but I'm not into older women. I'm sure you're a great catch, but—"

Mulberry roared with laughter. "You're adorable, but you're almost young enough to be my son. You're coming with me to Cat Alley. I've got the perfect cat waiting for you."

Chris shook his head, surprise in his eyes. "I'm not in the market for a cat. I'm just here to support Gabe and Rhyannon."

"I think it's a brilliant idea," I said. "There are loads of cats here who need homes, and you've got that huge bachelor pad all to yourself. I'm always telling you it needs some soul putting into it."

"Yeah, it doesn't need anything like that. And that's how I like it."

I shook my head. "Soulless with no personality?"

"Hey! It has personality."

"The walls are beige and you haven't hung a single picture since you moved in. How long has that been?"

Chris rubbed the back of his neck. "A while. It's set up just for me, though. There's no room for a cat."

"I've actually got two in mind for you," Mulberry said.

"Two cats! Lady, you've got the wrong person. I'll put another donation in the bucket if you like, but—"

"No! I can sense it. The time is right for you to have cats in your life." She grabbed hold of his elbow. "Come with me. I'll make the introductions."

I laughed as Chris was dragged away by Mulberry as she chatted to him and waved her arms in the air. "Is she always like that?"

"Pretty much. Mulberry can be a bit pushy, but her heart is in the right place. And she has this uncanny knack of being able to match people with the perfect cat. She does it time and time again. And she always knows when a new arrival is right for me to take in. She'll give me a call and tell me all about them. She's never made a bad decision yet when it comes to my fur babies."

"It sounds like she could be a Christmas angel, too," I said.

"Mulberry is the true angel at Forever Paws," Rhyannon said.

"I happen to think you're a pretty special angel as well." I kissed the tip of her nose. "Are you happy?"

"I think I'd burst if I was any happier." She gripped my hands and took a step back. "Gabe, you helped me realize what I've been missing. I... I never thought I was good enough to be loved."

"Rhyannon, no! That's not—"

"Hear me out. I thought I had enough with my volunteering and helping the cats. And it was great. I didn't even notice what I was missing out on until I met you again. You showed me that there are good men out there. Men with generous hearts and giving natures. Men I can trust, and most importantly, who love cats."

The adorable tilt of her head had my heart stuttering. "I haven't always been like this. And it takes a special woman to make me give up a car I've been drooling over for months."

She pressed a hand to my heart. "I still can't believe you did that. With the donations from tonight and what we've already raised, we can get started on installing the heating straight after Christmas. By the end of the year, we'll have a new heating system that'll provide heat in all the pens."

"And that's what's important. This place is important to you. Therefore, it's important to me." I tugged her closer. "And you helped me, too. You made me want to be generous and give to others. And you trusted me, even when Jessica made a play for me. You didn't even blink."

"Because we're in this together. And you've been nothing but honest with me." She placed a sweet kiss on my lips.

Donut yawned in my ear, before sliding down my chest and into my arms. He snuggled between the two of us, resting his butt in my hands and placing his front paws on Rhyannon's arms.

"Will you look at that," I said. "It's like he's joining us together. Tying a furry love knot between us so we're bonded for life."

"For life?"

"Isn't that what the sign says in your window, a cat is for life, not just for Christmas? The same goes for us. I want this forever. I want to be with you forever."

"I want that, too." Rhyannon's husky voice had my gaze going to her lips. "But let's take our time. Now we're together, we can really enjoy getting to know each other. And I need to make sure all my cats approve of you."

"Whatever you want. And I promise never to let you or your cats down." My heart was sure, but I'd happily take Rhyannon on as many diner dates as she wanted to make her certain she needed me forever.

"Meow?" Donut looked up at us before purring. He tilted his head my way and winked one eye.

"Huh! I didn't know cats winked."

"Only the special ones," Rhyannon said.

"Of course, he's special. Donut chose you."

"We chose each other," she said.

"Yeah, I reckon that's right. This is the best Christmas ever."

"Same here. I couldn't have asked for anything more," Rhyannon said.

I kissed her cheek before stroking Donut's head. "And it'll be the first of many."

Epilogue - 1 year later - Christmas Eve

Donut

"Okay, buddy, you remember the routine? When I whistle, you come into the kitchen." Gabe sat in front of me. The anxiety radiating off him was making my fur bristle, like I'd just rubbed against a nylon sweater.

I shuffled my butt closer and blinked my eyes. I knew the routine. We'd been practicing for a month. My part hadn't always gone well, but I knew how important this was to Gabe, so I'd do my best to get it right.

"You'll do great, buddy." His large, warm hand stroked down my back.

It hadn't been so long ago that I'd have cringed away and shut down in shock at his touch, but now I reveled in it. I felt secure in Gabe's arms. He never dropped me, never raised his voice, and always had a smile and a treat for me. He was my second favorite human in the whole world. We'd made the best decision when we'd picked Gabe to be with Rhyannon.

Ginger limped over and head bumped me in his intrusive, no clue about personal space way he always did.

I let him off the infraction. We were all excited to see how things would go this evening. Rhyannon would be back at any moment, and Gabe had spent all afternoon getting things ready.

We'd all had fun skating around on the cut out hearts he'd scattered in the hallway, creating a path for Rhyannon to follow. It wasn't until he'd enticed us away with a plateful of fresh chicken that he'd been able to make his final plans.

"This is it, boys and girls. What do you think she's going to say?" Gabe stood and rubbed his hands down the front of his best pair of jeans.

He only wore these on special occasions. And I'd heard Rhyannon say she wished he wore them more often because they made his butt look good.

I glanced at Ginger, and he flipped his tail. I returned the gesture. We both agreed, tonight was just what Rhyannon needed. And she'd say yes.

Gabe ran a hand over his hair and looked around the hallway.

I bumped my head against his leg in an attempt to reassure him.

Ginger did the same on the other leg, weaving around him and leaving behind a curtain of ginger fur.

"It's a good thing Rhyannon's so crazy about you." Gabe brushed off the fur. "It's a good thing I am, too." He stroked both our heads, then stiffened and his gaze shot to the door. "That's her car."

My tummy gave a lurch, suggesting a hairball was imminent, but I was fine. Rhyannon fed me salmon flavored paste several times a week to keep those pesky hairballs at a minimum. And this wasn't a hairball moment, this was a proposal moment.

"Everyone in their places." Gabe touched the end of my nose softly. "Whatever you do, don't lose that box."

I wiggled my head, trying to get him to see the little black box was attached to my collar, and it wasn't going anywhere. Even if a mouse popped out of a hole and raised its little fists in a challenge, I wouldn't be distracted. This was all about Rhyannon's happiness tonight.

Ginger speed-hopped away, and I wobbled into the lounge and hid behind the door.

Gabe's footsteps retreated into the kitchen, and then there was silence, apart from a loud sneeze from Fluffball. Even the house seemed to be holding its breath.

A key rattled in the front door, and my heart gave a little skip of excitement.

The gasp from Rhyannon's mouth had my whiskers twitching.

"What's all this?" Her tone was full of surprise.

I couldn't resist a peek around the side of the door. She'd placed her bags down and was staring at the hearts scattered across the wooden floor.

"Gabe, did you do this?" she called out.

On cue, Ginger limped into view.

"Hello, sweetie. Do you know what's going on?" Rhyannon reached down to stroke him, but he kept just out of reach, forcing her to walk across the hearts and head toward the kitchen where Gabe was waiting.

This was going so well, I wanted to squeak with excitement.

"What's wrong, Ginger? You usually love a cuddle as soon as I get home." Rhyannon hurried after him.

I snuck out from my hiding place and focused hard on keeping a straight line. Gabe had helped me master this by pointing out the lines on the floors where the boards fit, and I followed those. All I needed to do was keep looking at one of those lines and I'd go in the right direction.

It was going pretty decent, but the box attached to my collar wasn't helping my straight line walking. It was only small, but knocked me off balance a few times. I did a circle and was looking at my tail as I tried to set myself right.

Panic set in and I froze. I couldn't mess this up. I wouldn't let Rhyannon down. She had my heart, just like she had Gabe's. I wouldn't hurt that perfect little heart for all the salmon twizzles in the world.

I stopped, wriggled my shoulders, and waited for the world to stop tilting. Gabe was counting on me.

"Gabe, where are you?" Rhyannon called.

I flicked my gaze up to see Rhyannon in the kitchen, her back to me.

"Hey, beautiful." Gabe's warm, easy tone came from the kitchen. "You've been a long time. Were the stores busy?"

She unwrapped a thick scarf from around her neck and brushed melting snow off her hair. "They were. But you told me to enjoy myself, so I stopped for a coffee and a few sugar cookies on my way back."

There was that all too familiar kissing sound. I used to get a bit grossed out by that noise, but kissing made them happy, so I got used to it.

"I'm glad you had fun," he said.

"I did. But what's been going on here? And why are you dressed up? I didn't think we were going out tonight."

"We're not. Although we can if you like. Hold on a second, I've got something for you." Gabe whistled.

That was my cue. I focused on a line on the floor, put my head down and walked toward the kitchen.

Ginger sat to one side, a shrewd look on his face. Fluffball, Tom, Sinbad, and Jolene had appeared as well and watched me with a dazzling intensity. The pressure was definitely on.

"Donut! What have you got on your collar?" Rhyannon asked.

"Take a look," Gabe said. "There's something he thinks I should ask you."

"Is it one of those new tracking collars I keep talking about?" Rhyannon bent in front of me. She stroked my head, then twisted my collar until she saw the box. "Oh! This is a... a jewelry box."

Gabe looked at me and grinned as he knelt on one knee. "Rhyannon, there's something I have to ask you."

She turned, a breath shooting out of her and her hand going to her chest. She looked back at me and then at the box.

"You can open it," Gabe said. "It's for you. The cats have checked it out and they all approve."

"Is this for real?" she whispered.

Gabe's grin widened. He beckoned me over with his fingers, and I wobbled my way toward him. "Thanks, buddy. You did a perfect job. I knew you would."

I stayed where I was, letting him take the box, my chest swollen with pride. I'd done it. I'd help create this happy ending.

Gabe flipped open the box and extracted a beautiful, sparkling ring.

"Oh, Gabe! I didn't expect this." Rhyannon sounded so breathless I was worried she might pass out.

"You should have done," he said. "I hope I've made it clear that I don't want to be with anyone else. You're my always and forever. I want to spend the rest of my life making you as happy as possible."

"Gabe!" She'd covered her mouth with her hand, so the word was muffled.

Gabe looked at me and raised his eyebrows. "Shall I ask?"

I head-butted his knee. What was he waiting for?

"You're right. No more waiting. I've waited too long for my special someone. And aren't we all lucky to have found her?"

We all meowed and chirped our agreement. Gabe was a keeper.

"So, I just need to say, Rhyannon, will you marry me?" Gabe held the ring out in a hand that shook a fraction.

She squeaked, before flinging her arms around him and almost knocking him over. "Yes! Of course, I'll marry you."

This felt like a private moment, so I backed away and stopped beside Ginger. We exchanged an amused glance. Humans in love were so weird. But seeing Rhyannon hugging Gabe and laughing made my toe beans tingle with delight.

Rhyannon, the world's best human, was finally, truly happy. It wasn't the happiness she got from being with me and the other furries, but the kind of happiness she deserved.

Humans called it true love, and it seemed truly great to me.

I purred to myself and gave Ginger a lick on the head. Now our home was complete, and the true magic of Christmas was all around us.

About Author

♥

Karen Drew loves romance, gentle heroes who never give up on true love, and animals. Sweet romance, quirky pets, and happily ever afters fill her books.

When she's not writing, she's exploring the world of interesting flavors of tea, enjoying cake, and dreaming of new happily ever afters to delight readers.

Join her on Facebook for regular tea and cake updates, book news, and regular chats about all things animal:
www.facebook.com/karendrewauthor

Or join her newsletter and receive a **free** book:
https://BookHip.com/ZKJQFF

Also By

♥

12 Cats
Merry Christmas, Kitten
Joy to the Cats
Mistletoe and Meows

Furs Hill sweet romance
Love, Furballs, and Forever
Love, Pawprints, and Promises
Love, Happiness, and Hounds
Love, Kittens, and Kisses

If you enjoyed

Mistletoe and Meows

turn the page to read an extract from book one in
the Furs Hill series

LOVE, FURBALLS, AND FOREVER
ISBN: 978-1-915378-24-8

Chapter 1

♥

"You'll take this land over my dead body." Juliet Connelly's eyes tightened as her fingers clenched around the phone.

"There's no need to get hysterical. This is simply business." Bruce Jones's smug tone only irritated her further.

They'd been speaking for a few minutes, and Juliet was frazzled by the interaction.

"I'm not hysterical. No matter how many ways you sell this to me, Furs Hill isn't available to the developer." She'd had this conversation with Bruce a dozen times over the last eight weeks.

At first, he'd tried charming her. Then he'd tried to guilt trip her into believing the money they'd receive from the land sale could support more unwanted animals. He'd stopped the charm offensive after she'd told him to get lost in language that would make her mom blush. He deserved it. No one threatened to shut down Furs Hill Rescue Center.

"You must be exhausted from keeping that place afloat." Bruce's tone slid into conciliatory. "The sale will come with a healthy bonus payment for you. Obviously, you're the brains of the operation. We'll rely on you to see the smooth sale of the land through to completion."

"I'm not interested in your money," Juliet said. "Furs Hill has been helping abandoned animals for almost fifty years. It'll continue to do so for decades to come."

"Things change. The land that place is on is worth a fortune. We both know that. I've been upfront with you as to how much the developer is willing to pay. If it's not enough, you give me a number, and I'll go back to them. They want that land. My employer is extremely generous."

Juliet's gaze went to the picture laden wall in her cramped office. The wall was crowded with frames of different shapes and sizes showing the happy-ever-after stories that Furs Hill had achieved.

As the only no-kill shelter on the outskirts of Saffron Springs, Oregon, the charity often took in the more challenging cases. Time, money, and lashings of love were spent on the animals that people considered too broken to save. Not at Furs Hill. Every animal who came through the doors got the chance to find a happy home.

"I can tell you're wavering," Bruce said. "Perhaps an all-expenses paid team training event somewhere tropical and extravagant will encourage you to be open-minded. Anywhere you like. We have properties on every continent."

Juliet ground her teeth. "Not only are you suggesting I skim money off the top of this sale, you also want to bribe me with a vacation." She didn't have time for this. As center manager, Juliet looked after dozens of staff and ensured the smooth running of an always-busy operation that was open twenty-four hours a day.

"There's nothing illegal about any of that," Bruce said. "Those are our standard operating terms. What's your weakness, Juliet?"

"I don't have one."

"Everyone has a price. I'll find something you want more than that center."

"What I want is to end this call." Juliet's jaw unclenched as her gaze settled on the worn cardboard box that lived on the edge of her desk. The edges were scarred with tooth marks. The box was lined with soft bedding, and nestled in that bedding was the grumpiest elderly tabby cat Juliet had ever met.

Lady Pettypaw was a permanent resident of Furs Hill. After several failed rehoming attempts, thanks to her sullen nature and fast paws that swiped at anyone she didn't like, the cat had chosen a home that suited her. That home was Juliet's office, after she'd made the mistake of leaving an empty cardboard box on the desk.

Lady Pettypaw rarely left her box, and woe betide anyone who moved it. She had a particularly angry meow if she discovered her box gone.

Juliet was only half-listening as Bruce tried to justify the way he operated. He used phrases such as market value, an excellent opportunity, money to be made, and best for the animals. It all drifted through her thoughts and out again. He could have told her anything. Furs Hill was staying put.

When she'd first been approached by Hillview Homes with an offer to buy the twelve acres of land, Juliet was surprised but had politely declined.

She recognized the land had value, sitting less than ten miles from the prosperous small town of Saffron Springs, but to her, what already sat on the land was priceless.

The land had been gifted to the fledgling charity fifty years ago by an avid supporter of animal welfare. Since then, it had grown to include rehoming wings for cats and dogs, pens for other small furries—including rabbits and guinea pigs—a rehab and rehabilitation center, a training zone, and a quiet zone for new intakes.

"Miss Connelly, I appreciate your passion for animal welfare," Bruce said. "We'll ensure the animals are safely relocated. And, of course, my employer will make a generous donation to any charity of your choice."

"There's no need for that," she said sweetly. "The animals aren't going anywhere. Of course, if you'd like to make that donation directly to us, that will be wonderful. We'll put it to good use."

Bruce snorted. "I understand you're the manager, but you don't have complete control over what goes on at Furs Hill."

She stiffened in her seat. "What does that mean?"

"I know some of your trustees. Alfred Grimes is a golfing buddy, and my current CEO regularly has drinks with Patricia Landon. As members of your governing body, they'll have the final decision on what happens. It'll be easy for me to chat with them off the record and see what they think about the offer. I trust you aren't withholding this information from them? They won't appreciate being kept in the dark about something so important."

Juliet's temper flared. There was no point in shouting at this idiot. Although, it would make her feel better. Yelling would scare Lady Pettypaw, who was currently snuggled so deeply in her blanket that she could barely be seen, other than two dark brown ear tips.

"Mr. Jones, you may speak to any trustee you wish. They're all passionate about animals. I can assure you that they won't want to see one hundred and sixty homes scarring this beautiful site. You can offer any incentive you like, but you will fail."

"You'd be surprised," Bruce said. "With the right incentives, most people have a change of heart."

"Not at Furs Hill." Although Juliet's words sounded firm, a flicker of worry grew inside her. She'd worked in the banking industry for ten years and witnessed a number of under the table deals. People weren't incorruptible. Juliet hated to think anyone on the Board of Trustees at Furs Hill could be swayed by an attractive deal from the developer.

"I'll leave you with our most recent offer," Bruce said. "I don't want to go over your head on this matter, but make no mistake, I will if I have to. We will get that land. Our new homes are going on that plot."

"Not while I'm in charge," Juliet said.

"That can also change," Bruce said. "People come and go. Priorities alter. You're not as indispensable as you think you are. Good day, Miss Connelly."

She pulled the phone from her ear and glared at it. Now he was threatening to take away her job!

Juliet shook her head and dropped the phone on the desk.

Her gaze went to her computer screen, which showed the latest income reports. Worry churned inside her as she tugged on the ends of her hair. With the looming threat from the developer, she'd been keeping a close eye on the money coming into Furs Hill, to ensure there was no economic reason the trustees would welcome their offer.

The charity received regular small donations from thousands of supporters and some larger amounts from wealthy donors and charitable foundations.

She'd been expecting to see three large donations arrive in the accounts this week. So far, none of them had been deposited.

The trustees would notice this dip in income and ask questions. And if Bruce followed through and went straight to them and started planting doubts about stability and loss of income, the center could be at risk, especially if the offer to buy the land kept creeping up.

"We're not letting that happen, are we, Lady Pettypaw?" Juliet dipped her fingers into the box and rubbed the cat's head. She got a grumble for her effort.

Lady Pettypaw was a refined cat of an advanced age. She chose when and where she could be petted. Sometimes, she allowed a chin tickle. Other times, she would narrow her eyes as if daring you to even think you had the right to breathe the same air as her.

Risking one more tickle, and enjoying the feel of velvet fur and warm ears, Juliet refocused. It was time to find these donations.

She located the number for the Paws Hope Foundation and called them. Their donation could be delayed. It happened sometimes. Decisions were made later than planned, or money wasn't transferred due to a public holiday. There'd be a rational explanation for the funds not arriving.

Juliet tapped her fingers on the desk as she waited for the call to connect.

"Good morning. Paws Hope Foundation."

"Hi, I wonder if you can help me," Juliet said. "I'm calling from Furs Hill Rescue Center. We're expecting a donation from you, and it's yet to arrive. I'm just chasing it up. We have lots of hungry mouths to feed. They're all eager for your support."

"Let me see," the woman on the line said. "Did you say Furs Hill?"

"That's right."

"I have the minutes of our latest meeting in front of me. Your charity was mentioned." There was the sound of tapping fingers on the keyboard. "Ah! Bit of a problem. They decided not to award the money."

Juliet's breath caught in her throat. "Why? They seemed so positive about the application."

"You'll receive a letter outlining the reasons for the refusal."

"That money is so important to us. Is it too late to reverse the decision?"

"Never say never. There was some debate about the charity and if the donation should be given.

Your work is well-known to us. Everyone here is a supporter."

"Please, this support is crucial to Furs Hill. Can I get more information now? Or I can send a revised application if there was something that wasn't favored?"

The woman was silent for a few seconds. "One moment, I'll see if a trustee is available to speak with you. They will know more. I just take the notes."

"Thank you." Juliet's heart thudded at the thought of not getting that money. It was a donation of seventy thousand dollars. The money had been allocated to pay for staff and resources at the new rehab center that was about to open. Without the money, there would be a beautiful new building extension but nothing to go in it and no staff to work there.

"Connecting you now."

Juliet sucked in a breath and forced herself to remain calm.

"This is Daniel Braithwaite. Who am I speaking to?"

"Juliet Connelly. Thanks for taking my call. I believe there's a problem with the donation Paws Hope was planning to make to Furs Hill."

"Miss Connelly, I'm sorry to say that is correct."

"Is there something specific about our proposal you didn't like? When your colleague visited, he was very enthusiastic about our work."

"We all are, but we received worrying information about the stability of the charity just before our meeting."

Her stomach clenched, and her palms grew damp. "Furs Hill is stable. You've seen our last three years of accounts. We have a small surplus and plans for expansion."

Daniel sighed. "We debated giving you the donation for some time, but we must give our resources to charities that have a secure future. We can't give you money and then have you fold the next year. That would be wasteful."

"That won't happen. We're going nowhere," she said.

"Not according to an associate of mine," Daniel said. "I've heard that the center might be sold to make way for a new housing development."

Juliet winced as if she'd been punched in the gut. "That's not true."

"My source is reliable. The company seeking your land is a persistent one. They rarely fail to close a deal when they find a parcel of land they wish to build upon. I used to be in the development business myself, so I know how they operate."

"If you're referring to the interest shown by Hillview Homes, I've told them repeatedly, Furs Hill is here to stay."

"You can't guarantee that. Land such as yours is in big demand to meet future housing needs. They may make you an offer you can't refuse."

"We'll refuse all of their offers. The animals are the most important thing to us." Juliet felt queasy. She couldn't let this happen. "Please, reconsider your decision. That money is essential to our work."

"I'm sorry. The decision has been made. If, in eighteen months' time, the developer's demands have gone away, you're welcome to apply again. Until that threat has been removed, we won't accept any new requests for funding from Furs Hill."

Juliet sank in her seat, her eyes narrowed. So, this was how the developer would play the game. They were cutting off the charity's resources, trying to make them desperate enough to sell.

She didn't know whether to scream or cry. Instead, Juliet focused on breathing. She would handle this. She'd dealt with worse. "Thank you for your time."

Juliet ended the call and immediately rang the second charitable foundation who had yet to send their donation. Her heart sank as she received exactly the same response.

She had no clue how the developer had found out who Furs Hill had made financial requests to, but they'd talked three potential donors out of giving them money. Money they needed. Money for the animals.

Her gaze went back to the wall of furry faces in front of her. The charity had helped thousands of dogs, cats, and other small furries to find happy homes. Furs Hill was going nowhere, but without this money, Juliet wasn't sure where to turn next, especially if the developer kept dripping poison into people's ears about the stability of the charity.

There was a knock on the office door. The receptionist, Sandy Appleton, poked her head in. "Your visitor's here."

Juliet's brow wrinkled. "Who am I seeing?"

Sandy smiled. "Check your calendar. I put in the appointment. It's Carlisle Danvers."

"That name's familiar. Why is he here?" Juliet opened her calendar. Sure enough, there was the appointment. She rarely missed anything that was scheduled in her calendar, but Bruce had distracted her.

"Carlisle came to our last charity event. He gave a donation after we helped his sick cat. Selena set up the meeting." Sandy smiled and waggled her eyebrows. "Apparently, Mr. Danvers is a wealthy man. He's also very cute."

"Did you say wealthy?" Juliet blew out a breath. It was as if fate had stepped in just when she needed a helping hand.

"Yes. And gorgeous." Sandy grinned.

"He can be as gorgeous as he likes." Juliet wasn't looking for gorgeous. She needed a backup plan to prevent the developer causing any more trouble. Carlisle Danvers could be her savior. "Thanks, Sandy. I'll be out in a second."

The tension seeped from Juliet's shoulders as she stood and smoothed her hands down her pants. She needed to seal this deal. The center needed this. The animals needed Carlisle to fall in love with them and help them out of this problem.

She checked her reflection in the compact mirror in her purse, ran a hand through her blonde hair, and smiled to herself. She'd charm Mr. Danvers into making a donation. The center would be just fine.

Love, Furballs, and Forever is available in paperback and ebook.
ISBN: 978-1-915378-24-8

www.ingramcontent.com/pod-product-compliance
Lightning Source LLC
Chambersburg PA
CBHW030835200726
48285CB00007B/2446